UNCHAPERONED!

And then—directly in front of his eyes, like a lowly caterpillar shedding its cocoon—Elinor Dalrymple metamorphosed into the most glorious painted lady he had ever been privileged to see!

He could feel his body responding to the stimuli of Elly's appearance, to the sweet violet scent of her hair as it billowed in the breeze off the Channel, to the moist sweetness of her mouth as she smiled up at him with all the guileless invitation of a first-time strumpet.

Her hands on her hips, her entire stance daring him to speak, he heard her say, "Well, John, do you still believe we are in no need of a chaperone?"

The little tart! She was baiting him, deliberately urging him to commit an action that could be seen as nothing less than a marriage-mandatory compromise of her reputation. He'd like to slap her silly. He'd like to grab her by the shoulders and—and kiss her until she begged for mercy!

Kasey Michaels is the *New York Times* and *USA Today* bestselling author of more than sixty books. She has won the Romance Writers of America RITA Award and the *Romantic Times* Career Achievement Award for her historical romances set in the Regency era, and also writes contemporary romances for Silhouette and Harlequin Books.

The Dubious
Miss Dalrymple

TORONTO • NEW YORK • LONDON
AMSTERDAM • PARIS • SYDNEY • HAMBURG
STOCKHOLM • ATHENS • TOKYO • MILAN • MADRID
PRAGUE • WARSAW • BUDAPEST • AUCKLAND

ISBN 0-373-51184-1

THE DUBIOUS MISS DALRYMPLE

Printed in U.S.A.

PROLOGUE

"HAVE YOU HEARD the news?"

Lord Blakestone lowered his newspaper to glare overtop it at the excited young man who had dared to intrude on his peace. Heaven knew he got precious little of it these days. "I *read* the news when I require an infusion of knowledge, Hopwood," he told the fellow in crushing tones meant to depress this increasing familiarity that was fast making Boodle's coffee room too common for words. "If I wished the day's happenings bellowed at me, I would sit in my own house and let my wife's dear, beloved mother natter me to death."

Hopwood was instantly cast down, but he was by no means to be counted out. He'd come directly from Bond Street, where tongues had been wagging nineteen to the dozen, and he'd be damned for a dolt if he was going to allow this chance to elevate his consequence here at Boodle's—a club he had stumbled into because of his parentage, and not his own standing or even inclination—to be stomped on by a pompous blowfish like Blakestone. "But—but I just heard. It's the most incredible thing! Lord Hythe is dead!"

Blakestone tossed his newspaper to the floor in an untidy heap, grumbling something about the servants being reminded to take better care when pressing the pages so that they would refold themselves automatically when the dratted thing was no longer required.

After venting his spleen on both the hapless newspaper and the overworked Boodle's servants (who were undoubtedly at that moment boiling coins somewhere in the bowels of the club so that the members should not have to smudge themselves by handling dirty money), he looked up at Hopwood and inquired shortly: "I don't believe it. Wythe? Wythe's dead?"

Hopwood shook his head vigorously. As audiences went, Blakestone appeared to be a poor choice. "No, no. Not Wythe. Hythe."

"Don't correct your betters, you miserable scamp. I say, Freddie!" Lord Blakestone called to Lord Godfrey, who had just entered the coffee room. "Have you heard the latest? Dreadful news. Wythe is dead."

"No!" Lord Godfrey ejaculated, pressing a hand to his chest, as if to be sure his own heart was still ticking along normally. He and Wythe were much of the same age. "How did it happen?"

Lord Blakestone waved an arm imperiously, summoning a servant and ordering another, freshly pressed, newspaper. "Damned if I know, old man. What do I look like, Freddie? A bleeding newsboy? Ask this puppy here. He seems to be hot to spread the gossip. Finally!" he groused, snapping the freshly pressed newspaper out of the servant's hand. "Took you twelve seconds too long, my fine fellow. You'll never get ahead in life lollygagging, y'know."

Lord Godfrey turned to Hopwood, who was leaning against a heavy mahogany table and most probably wondering what he had done to deserve membership to a snake pit such as Boodle's. "Corny says to ask you, whoever you are. So? Well, speak up, young man. What happened to Wythe? I saw him just last week at Tatt's, full of piss and vinegar as ever. Dead, you say? How'd it happen? Apoplexy? He was getting on, wasn't he—at least ten years my senior, I'm sure.''

''Five your junior,'' Lord Blakestone corrected heartlessly, turning the page to check on the latest news of Napoleon Bonaparte's bloodletting on the Continent. ''You're looking pale, Freddie. It's all that running about you do with that warbler from Covent Garden. Not seemly in a man your age—nor smart, now that I think about it. Best sit down before you join Wythe below ground.''

Hopwood felt an almost overwhelming urge to pull at his hair and scream, or possibly even throw something—Lord Blakestone's dusty wig was the first object that came to mind. ''Not Wythe, sir—Hythe. He was young, in his prime. I was just taking the air on Bond Street when I heard the news. He was lost overboard from his yacht in a storm or something. Near Folkestone, I think.''

Lord Godfrey subsided into a burgundy leather wing chair, glaring impotently at Lord Blakestone, his agitated brain taking in information only as it pertained to him. ''A yacht? I didn't know Wythe could afford to keep a yacht.'' As he couldn't show any real anger toward Lord Blakestone, whose social connections were considerably powerful, he directed his fury at a man who could no longer hurt him. ''Y'know what—bloody stingy, that's what Wythe was. A yacht! Never took me up on the thing.''

Goaded, or so he felt, past all bearing, Hopwood opened his mouth and shouted—just as a half dozen

worse-for-liquor gentlemen sitting in the dirty end of
the room exploded in mirth over some joke or other:
"Not Wythe, you feather-witted old nincompoops!
Hythe! Hythe!"

While neither Lord Blakestone nor Lord Godfrey
paid so much as a jot of attention to the red-faced
young man bellowing ridiculousness within four feet
of their ears, they were attracted to the sounds of mer-
riment across the room, and immediately longed to
join in the fun. Looking back and forth to each other
across the table that separated their matching burgundy
leather wing chairs, the two lords scrambled to their
feet, knowing their gossip would be a sure entry to the
group.

As they walked toward the small gathering of gentlemen, they called out in unison, "Have you heard?
It's all over town. It's the strangest thing. Wythe's
dead!"

"Not Wythe, you paper-skulled asses. *Hythe!* Alastair Lowell, Fourteenth Earl of Hythe, and a damned
fine gentleman." Hopwood pushed the discarded
newspaper to the floor and collapsed into Lord Blakestone's abandoned chair, giving up the fight. "Oh,
what does it matter anyway?" he soothed himself.
"The fellow's still dead, ain't he?"

A MEMORIAL SERVICE was held three weeks later at
Seashadow, the Hythe seat in Kent, with several of the
late Earl's friends making the trip down from London
in the fine spring weather to pay their respects—although it was rather awkward that there was no body
to neatly inter in the family mausoleum.

"His bright light lies asleep with the fishes," the

vicar had intoned gravely upon mounting the steps to the lectern, these depressing words heralding an hour-long sermon that went on to graphically describe the water fate of Alastair Lowell's earthly remains until a none too discreet cough from Miss Elinor Dalrymple—sister of the new Earl—caused the man to reel in his tongue just as he was about to utter the words "putrid flesh" for a seventh time.

The number of fashionable young ladies of quality (as well as a colorful spattering of beautiful but not quite so eligible women) among the mourners would have cheered Alastair Lowell no end had he been privileged to see them—and so said his friends as they paid their respects to the new Earl and his solemn-faced sister before hastily departing the crepe-hung chapel for some decidedly more cheerful atmosphere.

"Made a muff of it," Leslie Dalrymple, the new Earl, said tragically, watching from the portico as the last traveling coach pulled out of the yard, leaving him to deal with a dining room piled to the chandeliers with uneaten food. "Ain't congenial, y'know. Never were."

"Nonsense, darling," Elinor Dalrymple consoled her brother, patting his thin cheek. "You were all that is gracious, and your eulogy, although understandably brief, as you had never met our cousin, was everything it could be. The late Earl, rest his soul, merely attracted those of his own, irresponsible ilk—considering that it is rumored our departed cousin was deep in his cups the night of his fatal accident. Doubtless they're all off now to carouse far into the night, toasting their fallen friend and otherwise debauching themselves."

Leslie shook his blonde, shaggy head, dismissing her assumption that he blamed himself for his guests' hasty departure. "Not me, Elly. You. You're the one routed them—what with your starchy ways. Scared them off, that's what you did. Besides, black does not become you. Don't understand it, as you're blonde and all, but there it is. I do wish you wouldn't persist in wearing such dark colors."

Elinor looked up at her brother, who, although three years her junior, stood a full foot higher than she. "Thank you, Leslie," she rejoined calmly, slipping her arm through his. "You have truly made my day. Now, would you be so kind as to join me in the dining room? I wouldn't wish for all that food to go to waste."

The pair entered the house to see that the Biggs family, clad in their Sunday finery, was lined up at attention in the enormous three-story-high hall, obviously in preparation of meeting the late Earl's mourners.

Nine heads turned toward the doorway as Leslie and Elinor stepped across the threshold; nine necks craned forward to look past their masters for the horde of diners about to push their knees beneath the late Earl's table and eat their heads off; nine pairs of sky-blue eyes widened as Elinor closed the door firmly on the spring sunshine, and nine mouths split into wide, anticipatory grins as their new mistress announced that the Biggses would just have to discover some way to dispose of the bound-to-be-ample remnants of the funeral feast.

Billie Biggs shifted Baby Willie, her youngest, on her hip and took one step forward. "Chased 'em off, did ya?'' she asked in her deep, booming voice that reached all the way up to the rafters. "Good for you, missy. Never saw a sorrier-lookin' bunch in m'life. They'd have ate us out of house an' home before we knew which way to look. Come on, children—best get outta those duds afore ya ruin 'em."

Each Biggs child obediently stepped forward in turn, to either bow or drop curtsies to the Dalrymples before leaving the hall.

Little Georgie, who helped his father in the kitchens (and the eldest at eighteen, though definitely not the brightest), tugged at his forelock and bowed his immense frame low, saying only, "Daft sort of party," before shuffling toward the scullery—his mother's absentminded cuff across the top of his head hurrying him on his way.

Lily, sixteen, a very pretty girl who served as upstairs maid, made an elaborate curtsey to Leslie—ignoring Elinor's presence—and headed for the staircase, her skirts twitching side to side as provocatively as she dared allow in her mother's presence.

Fifteen-year-old Harry, who worked in the stables, approached the Dalrymples and offered his condolences in a polite voice before passing behind them and through the front door, intent upon returning to the stable yard to check on a mare ready to drop her foal.

Elinor, whose new shoes were pinching her unmercifully, resigned herself to accepting the mumbled condolences of Iris, aged ten, Rosie, eight and one-half, and Bobby, a five-year-old cherub whose tumbling curls and intelligent eyes had, at first sight, prompted Elinor to believe Billie Biggs had played her husband, Big George, false at least once.

Finally, with Billie shooing the younger children in front of her with her immense white apron while reminding the Dalrymples to hurry to the table before the food got cold, the hall was emptied of all but Elinor and her brother.

"Lovely people," Leslie said, waving to Baby Willie as the child dangled backwards over his mother's shoulder, all ten fingers stuck in his wet mouth. "So kind, so caring."

Elinor looked at her brother askance. "Leslie," she intoned coldly, "the Biggses are not our house guests. They are the sum total of the late Earl's idea of a servant force on this estate—other than the farm laborers and such. Big George cooks because Billie can't boil water without burning it—although he told me the other day that it suits him fine anyway because she keeps a neat house and can make babies. Harry is a good worker, but Little George is a complete loss. Lily is ripe to seduce anything in long pants, while Rosie, Bobby, and Baby Willie are too young to do much more than eat their heads off and take up space—although I must admit Iris shows promise."

Leslie was immediately apprehensive. "You don't mean to turn them off, do you, Elly?"

Elinor shook her head and sighed. "No, Leslie," she soothed wearily, "I don't mean to turn them off. Truthfully, the estate was running quite smoothly when we arrived, so I see no need to change anything. It's just—it's just that it's so depressing. I have nothing to *do*, Leslie. That boisterous woman and her gaggle of children have made me totally superfluous!"

Leslie was immediately all concern—for himself. "You—you wouldn't leave me, Elly, would you? I mean, I depend on you terribly—always have. Besides, you promised Papa you'd always take care of me." His green dreamer's eyes brightened as a thought hit him. "Tell you what, Elly. You can be in charge of my studio. That should keep you busy. I promise to be as messy as possible."

Elinor looked up at her brother, sure she could see a betraying tear in the corner of his left eye, and her heart softened. At three and twenty, she had long ago resigned herself to caring for her younger brother.

"Of course I would never leave you, darling," she assured him, patting his hand. "Where would I go? I was just being silly—thinking only of myself. I should be jumping through hoops at our good fortune, not complaining that fate has made us wealthy and comfortable. Three weeks ago I didn't know where our next quarter's rent was coming from—and today you are the Fifteenth Earl of Hythe, and so deep in the pocket, we shall never have to concern ourselves about money again. I shall just have to educate myself in the pastimes of the idle rich, that's all."

Leslie smiled, his fears banished. "That's settled then," he pronounced happily, secure once more in the comfortable cotton wool his sister had kept him in for as long as he could remember. "Shall we go in to luncheon? I want to get back to my studio before the light leaves me." Walking three paces ahead of his sister, who only shook her head in resigned good humor as she brought up the rear, Leslie began to expound on his latest project—a painting of a spotted dog, as viewed by a flea—all thoughts of the late Earl and his flighty cronies forgotten.

VISITORS TO THE SEAPORT city of Folkestone, when not worried about Bonaparte's threats of imminent invasion from the French coastline that was so close it was often visible with the naked eye, could amuse themselves by taking walking tours along the Leas, a grassy expanse on the top of the cliff that looked upon the Strait of Dover, or, on less balmy days, by strolling the wooded paths on the face of the cliff and the Undercliffe.

Few people, however, chose to walk much beyond the quaint and irregular streets of the oldest section of town to the most remote, windswept beach, and the odd, derelict cottage that huddled against the base of the cliff. There were stories about this cottage—blood-chilling stories told late at night to visitors as they sat in cozy inn parlors, rubbing mugs of mulled ale between their hands.

It seemed that a giant lived in the cottage, an immense, growling ogre who—if anyone were ever so foolish as to approach him—would crack that poor unfortunate's skull like an eggshell with his great club as soon as look at him! The good people of Folkestone cut a wide path around the Ogre of the Undercliffe, and even the military, customs officers, revenue men, and smugglers showed no interest in routing the ogre from his lair.

The cottage was small, but with high ceilings—probably to better accommodate the ogre's great height—and was most likely composed of a single, irregularly shaped room that served as kitchen, sitting room, and bedroom. The ocean served as the ogre's privy. Although even the most modest cottages in Folkestone boasted milky-paned glass windows, the ogre's three small windows were hung with oiled rags and black paper, so that no one could even boast of actually having seen inside the darkened cottage. They only knew it was a place they would rather not ever find themselves near on a moonless night.

It was to this unnatural darkness that the man awoke, at first only for a few moments, his mind unclear, his body racked with pain and fever, before slipping once more into a merciful oblivion where the smell of dog and sweat and damp and old meat could not find him.

The man had dreams as he lay on the hard cot, dreams that included a gigantic, hovering beast who could only be the Gatekeeper of Hell; although why the Gatekeeper of Hell would be feeding him snail tea in barley water was for the moment past his power's of comprehension.

As time went on—be it hours or days or weeks, the man did not know—the most annoying thing about his current position was the grating sound of an unoiled wheel that seemed to be constantly in motion. In the end, it was just this sound that brought the man to full consciousness, and he propped his weak body up on one elbow to squint through the darkness in search of the source of the sound.

"That explains the smell of dog," he pronounced blankly, looking at last to the crooked fireplace and the antiquated dogspit that was cut into the wall beside the stones. As the dog ran inside the wheel, chasing a pitifully small marrow bone that hung suspended just out of reach, the spit in the fireplace turned, allowing the unrecognizable joint of meat to cook evenly over the fire, basting in its own juices.

The man sniffed at the air tentatively a time or two, trying to recognize the meat by its smell, then looked to the slowly trotting canine. "Not a close relative, I trust?" he asked the mutt facetiously before collapsing once more onto the hard cot.

He hurt like the very devil, from the top of his pounding head to the tip of his toes, but the pain told him that he was alive, and he supposed he should be grateful for small favors. He coughed, and that action brought on more pain in his chest and throat. "Dog sick," he said, not bothering to excuse himself to the mutt.

Lifting a hand to his face, he touched a considerable growth of beard, which told him that he had been in the cottage a long time—although how he had gotten here, he could not remember. As a matter of fact, the last thing he did remember was taking the air on the deck of his yacht, the *Lark,* as it lay at anchor just off Folkestone.

Before setting sail he had endured a rather boring, if profitable, evening onshore at cards, his three casually met companions having proved to be as dullwitted at faro as they were in the art of conversation, so that it had not bothered him overmuch that he had pushed away from the table the big winner, leaving the other gentlemen to commiserate with one another over their collective run of bad luck.

Walking to the rail as the yacht headed out to sea, he had spent a few idle moments trying to make out the mist-softened shoreline in the still dark sky of early morning before turning in—his reminiscences stopped there as the full realization of what had happened finally hit him.

"I was pushed!" he shouted—startling the underfed hound into ceasing his endless walk on the wheel. "I was conked on the noggin like some wretch set upon by a press gang—and then tossed overboard as if I were so much garbage! I can even remember the feel of the water closing over my head! God's teeth, but I'd give half my fortune to know which one of the filthy bastards did it!"

He turned on the cot, forcing his bare feet to find purchase on the uneven packed-dirt floor of the cottage, and rose, nearly toppling backward as his physical weakness threatened to overcome his resolve to get himself back to civilization as fast as possible so that he could shoot somebody.

Only then did he realize that he was naked as a jaybird, with his clothing nowhere in sight. He stood in the dim light cast by the small fire, his rumpled blonde hair and fuzzy beard glowing golden in the glow, searching out the dim corners of the small cottage for any sign of his belongings.

A sense or urgency overcame him, giving him new strength. He had to be gone, had to seek help, had to discover who had pushed him—and why. Stumbling to one of the rag-covered windows, he ripped the material away and looked out across a rocky beach to where the surf was pounding against the shore. He looked back at the interior of the cottage, which hadn't been improved by the addition of a little daylight and fresh air.

Where was he? The place was a hovel; there was

no other word for it. This was no Kentish farmer's cottage. It was too close to the sea, for one thing. Could some fisherman have plucked him from the Channel? No, there were no nets drying outside in the sun, no harbor from which to launch a boat. He swallowed hard. He had to be in a smuggler's hideaway. It was the only answer.

"Probably holding me for ransom," he thought aloud, the pounding in his head threatening to send him back to the cot to mewl like a wounded sheep. "I wonder how much an Earl brings on the open market these days. Damn your shaky legs, Alastair Lowell, you've got to find something to wear and get the blazes out of here before the baddies get back!"

Just as Alastair was becoming desperate enough to consider draping himself in the tattered blanket that had covered him, the door to the hovel burst open. A wide shaft of sunlight sliced through the cottage, nearly blinding him, to be followed by a sudden and nearly total eclipse as the doorway was filled with the largest man he had ever seen.

"Hell's Gatekeeper!" Alastair breathed incredulously, involuntarily backing up until the edge of the cot caught him behind the knees and he sat down, covering his nakedness with the blanket. He knew he hadn't led the most exemplary of lives, but had he really merited this?

The giant advanced into the room, his huge head tipped inquisitively to one side as he looked at his guest, before his attention was distracted by something near the fireplace. He turned slowly toward the fireplace and growled deep in his throat. The dog, which had been curled up asleep at the bottom of the wheel, leapt to his feet and began running as fast as he could, the singed joint on the spit spinning about so rapidly that hot meat juice flew off it to sizzle against the stones of the hearth.

The giant grumbled in satisfaction, turning his attention once more to his guest. Advancing toward Alastair, he reached into his pocket and withdrew a greasy piece of much-folded paper and extended it to the smaller man.

"For me?" Alastair asked, hating the slight tremor in his voice. "You want me to read this?" The ogre nodded. "All right," the Earl said, gingerly accepting the scrap of paper. He looked up into the larger man's face, searching for some sign of intelligence. "I'm going to have to get up now, and move closer to the window to get some light. Is that all right with you? Good."

Alastair, the tattered blanket wrapped about his muscular frame like a toga, moved slowly toward the small window—doing his utmost not to make any disaster-causing sudden movements. "I'm Alastair Lowell, by the by," he said, making what he hoped was idle conversation as he unfolded the paper. "I'm the Earl of Hythe—which should not be too far from here, unless I somehow ended up on the wrong side of the Channel. *Parlez vous français,* friend ogre? No? Well, that's some small relief. All right, let me see what this says."

He read for a few moments, then looked up at the giant, who was hovering just a mite too close for comfort. "Hugo, is it?"

The giant nodded vigorously, a large smile cracking his face to expose a childish, gap-toothed grin. He slammed one hamlike fist against his barrel chest and growled low in his throat as if repeating his name.

"Uh-huh," Alastair said dryly. "Obviously Hugo. And this letter was written by your mother—dictated from her deathbed, actually, to someone who wrote it for her. How touching." He lowered his head to read the remainder of the short note. "Good God!" he exclaimed, looking up at Hugo, then down at the note once more. "Cut out your tongue? I can't believe it. Why in bloody hell would anybody want to—"

Hugo's left hand came down heavily on Alastair's shoulder, nearly buckling the Earl's knees. *"Aaarrgh,"* the giant groaned, opening his cavernous mouth to let Alastair view the damage for himself.

"Yes, indeed," the Earl concluded quickly, trying not to gag, "it's gone, all right. My condolences. Your mother says you're a good boy, Hugo, and that I should be nice to you. You're seven feet tall if you're an inch, old man. I'd like to meet the fellow who wouldn't be nice to you. Besides, unless I miss my guess, you saved my life."

Nodding his head several times, Hugo stepped back to begin an elaborate pantomime Alastair believed was meant to depict Hugo's daring rescue at sea. As the performance took some time, and the Earl was beginning to feel slightly giddy from being on his feet so long, it wasn't too many minutes before Alastair could feel the small room begin to swirl in front of his eyes.

The giant, apparently sensing Alastair's imminent collapse, broke off his performance to scoop the smaller man into his arms and lay him gently on the cot. His movements swift and economical, he had a meal of meat, thin broth, and boiled potatoes in front of Alastair before another ten minutes had passed, and he fed this to the patient from his own spoon, grumbling compliments for every bite of stringy meat Alastair swallowed.

Later, after watching Hugo wash the plates in a bucket of seawater he had carried into the cottage, and while the spit dog hungrily wolfed down the remnants of the meal, Alastair, his strength at last beginning to return, began a fact-finding conversation with his nurse-savior.

"How long have I been here, Hugo?" he asked as the giant unearthed the Earl's clothing from a small chest near the hearth.

Hugo held up three fingers.

"Three days? No, my beard is too long for that. Three weeks?" Hugo nodded his head in agreement. "Good God—the whole world must think me dead! Hugo—do you have a newspaper?"

The giant looked puzzled for a moment, then removed one gigantic wooden clog and pulled out the folded layers of newspaper that served as a cushion for his feet. Alastair accepted it gingerly, unfolding it with the tips of his fingers to see that the newspaper was six months out-of-date.

"Thank you, friend, but I fear I need something more recent than this," he said politely, quickly returning the paper, which Hugo replaced inside the clog. "We'll need money. Did I have any money with me? I should have—I was a big winner, as I recall, and hadn't as yet gone to my cabin to change out of my evening dress. But no, doubtless the man who hit me made sure to empty my pockets before dumping me overboard—why else would he bother with the exercise at all? I should have known that at least one of them would prove to be a poor loser. Good Lord, Hugo, I think I'm babbling.''

Within moments Hugo had laid a considerable sum of money in Alastair's lap, amazing the Earl with his honesty. The man couldn't have spent so much as a single copper on himself the whole time the Earl was unconscious. But, relieved as he was to see the money, it also seemed to eliminate his disgruntled gambling companions as possible suspects in his ''murder.''

Counting out a hundred pounds, Alastair handed it to Hugo, who refused to take it. ''Here, here, man, don't be silly. I owe you my life. Besides, I want you to go into the nearest town and buy every newspaper you can find. Where am I anyway, Hugo? East or west of Folkestone? West? Good. That means I can't be more than a stone's toss from Hythe—and Seashadow. That fits my plan exactly—did I fail to mention that I have a small plan building in my head? Tell me, my large friend, would you like to be a part of it?''

''Aaarrgh!'' Hugo agreed, clapping his hands.

''Good for you, Hugo, and welcome aboard! All right, let's get down to cases. I'll need some clothes— nothing too fancy, just a shirt and breeches, and perhaps a vest and hat. Oh, yes, I'll need smallclothes and shoes as well. The salt water has made my own clothes unwearable, even if you were so kind as to wash them. Do you think you can take care of that for me? Of course you can. You're very intelligent, aren't you, Hugo? Your mother said you are.''

Hugo's gap-toothed grin was curiously touching.

''I'll need paper, and pen and ink, of course,'' Alastair added, thinking aloud. ''I should think I'll want to get word to that Captain Wiggins fellow in the War Office that I'm still alive. He may prove useful. But I don't think I would wish the knowledge of my survival to go beyond him for the moment." He looked across the room at Hugo, then smiled. "Not much fear of that, is there?" he joked darkly, and Hugo's grin appeared once more.

"Yes," Alastair said, smiling genuinely for the first time since waking to find himself in the cottage, "this could prove to be extremely interesting."

CHAPTER ONE

THE KENTISH COAST had long been considered the gateway to England, an island empire whose six thousand miles of coastline were its best defense as well as its greatest weakness.

The Romans had landed along the Kentish coast, followed by the Germanic tribes that were united under Egbert, the "First King of the English." Alfred the Great, England's first great patron of learning, was sandwiched somewhere between Egbert and William the Conqueror, followed by the Plantagenets, the Tudors, the Stuarts, the terrible, tiresome, homegrown Cromwell, and finally, the House of Hanover and its current monarch, George III.

The king, blind and most decidedly mad, was not aware that his profligate, pleasure-seeking son had been named Regent, which was probably a good thing, for the knowledge just might have proven to be the death of poor "Farmer George"—but that is another story. More important was the fact that another adventurous soul was once again contemplating the Kentish coast with hungry eyes.

Napoleon Bonaparte, ruler of all Europe, had amassed the Grande Armée, his forces surpassing the ancient armies of Alexander, Caesar, Darius, and even Attila. He had set his greedy sights on England early in his campaign to conquer the world, although pressing matters on the Peninsula and to the east (where the Russians and their beastly winter had proved disastrous to the Little Colonel) had kept him tolerably busy and unable to launch his ships across the Channel. This did not mean that the English became complacent, believing themselves invincible to attack from the French coast.

Quite the contrary.

Martello Towers, an ambitious string of lookout posts built on high ground from Hythe to Eastbourne, were still kept munitioned and manned by vigilant soldiers of His Majesty's forces. Dressed in their fine red jackets, the soldiers stood at the high, slitted windows of the grey stone cylindrical towers, their glasses trained on the sea twenty-four stupefying hours a day. In their zeal to protect their shores, the English had even dug the Royal Military Canal between Rye and Appledore, optimistically believing that it would give them an extra line of defense from the Froggies.

Five great seaports—called the Cinque Ports—lined the southeast coast, at Hastings, Dover, Sandwich, Romney, and Hythe, with the towns of Rye and Winchelsea vying with them for prominence, and these too had garrisons of soldiers at the ready.

All this vigilance, all this preparedness, the Peninsula Campaign, and the Russian winter—added to the fact that the Strait of Dover, also referred to as "England's Moat," was not known for its easy navigability—had proved sufficient in keeping Bonaparte from launching his soldiers from Boulogne or Calais.

It was not, alas, sufficient in preventing inventive English smugglers from accumulating small fortunes plying their trade from Margate to Bournemouth, almost without intervention.

Using long-forgotten sea lanes, the smugglers, known as the "Gentlemen," did a roaring trade in untaxed medicine, rope, spices, brass nails, bridal ribbons, brandy, silk—even tennis balls. So widespread was the smuggling, and so accomplished were the Gentlemen, that even the Comptroller of the Foreign Post Office sanctioned the practice, as it brought French newspapers and war intelligence reports to the island with greater speed and reliability than any other, more conventional methods.

But, the Comptroller's protestations to one side, there were the Customs House officers to be considered. The smugglers may have been helping the war effort in some backhanded way, but they were also making the customs and revenue officers a redundant laughingstock, as the flow of contraband into England was fast outstripping the amount of legal, taxable cargo landed on the docks.

Many customs officers, loyal and hardworking, employed the King's men in forays against the smugglers. Many more did not. A few slit throats, a few bludgeoned heads—these were ample inducement for most customs officers to keep their noses tucked safely in their ale mugs on moonless nights, when the Gentlemen were apt to be out and about. Besides enhancing the possibility of living to a ripe old age, turning one's head was a good way for customs officers to increase their meager salaries, for the smugglers were known to be extremely generous to those who were good to them.

Popular sentiment as well was on the side of the

Gentlemen, whose daring at sea demanded admiration—and supplied the locals with a wide variety of necessities and luxuries without the bother of the recipients having to pay tax on the goods.

As late as July of 1805, Lord Holland, during a Parliamentary Debate, conceded that: "It is impossible to prevent smuggling.... All that the Legislature can do is to compromise with a crime which, whatever laws may be made to constitute it a high offence, the mind of man can never conceive as at all equalling in turpitude those acts which are breaches of clear, moral virtues."

All in all, it would be easy to believe that a, for the most part, comfortable bargain had been struck between the Gentlemen and the rest of the populate, but that was not the case. As the war dragged along, the unpaid taxes on contraband goods were, by their very absence, depleting the national treasury and war coffers, making the customs officers the butt of scathing lectures from their superiors in London.

The coastal forces, made up mostly of young men who had joined the military for the fun—the "dash" of the thing—only to be denied the clash of battle with the French, were itching to do battle with anyone. The Gentlemen and their nocturnal escapades were just the thing to liven up the soldiers' humdrum existence.

But most important, the Gentlemen, who were extremely profit-oriented, were lamentably not the most loyal of the King's subjects. Contraband was contraband, and money was money, no matter whose hand had held it last. Along with the spices and brandy and silk, there was many a French spy transported across

England's Moat, carrying secrets that could conceivably bring down the empire.

All this had served to complicate the Gentlemen's position, and by 1813 the many small dabblers in the art of smuggling had called it a day, and the majority of the contraband was brought to the shores by highly organized, extremely unlovely gangs of cutthroats, villains, and sundry other souls not averse to committing crimes "equalling in turpitude those acts which are breaches of clear, moral virtues."

THERE WAS A LONG, uncomfortable silence in the main drawing room of Seashadow, broken only by the light snoring of the napping Mrs. Biggs, whose impressed services as vigilant chaperone of Elinor Dalrymple's reputation left much to be desired.

"That was a most edifying dissertation, Lieutenant Fishbourne—even if the bits about Cromwell and the Regent did not necessarily relate to the Kentish coast. But it begs me now that you have concluded—you have concluded, haven't you?—to ask how all this pertains to me," Elinor Dalrymple inquired wearily as she poured the young man a second cup of tea—for his lengthy, dry-as-dust dissertation on the history of England and smuggling must surely have caused him to become quite parched. "Or should I say—how does all of this pertain to Seashadow? Surely you haven't had reports of smuggling or spying along our beaches?"

Lieutenant Jason Fishbourne, attached to the Preventive Service by the Admiralty and stationed these past eighteen months in the port of Hythe, leaned forward across the low serving table to utter confidentially, "Have you ever heard of the Hawkhurst Gang, Miss Dalrymple?"

Elly's voice lowered as well, one slim white hand going to her throat protectively, as if she expected it to be sliced from ear to ear at any moment. "The Hawkhurst Gang? But they are located near Rye, aren't they—if, indeed, that terrible gang is still in existence."

The Lieutenant sat back, smiling, as he was convinced he had made his point. "There are *many* gangs about, Miss Dalrymple," he intoned gravely. "Each one more bloodthirsty and ruthless than the next, I'm afraid. And yes, madam, I do suspect that one of them is operating in this area—very much so in this area."

Elly swallowed hard. Smugglers operating near Seashadow? Spies? And she had been walking the beach every day—sometimes even at dusk. Why, she could have stumbled upon a clutch of them at any time!

"What—what do you wish for us to do?" she asked the Lieutenant, who now commanded her complete attention. "We have only been here a few weeks, since just before the memorial service for the late Earl, as a matter of fact, but we intend to be contributing members of the community. I, in fact, have been searching for a project to occupy my time. Could I serve as a lookout of sorts, do you suppose?"

"Indeed, no, madam, I should not dream of putting you in any danger." Lieutenant Fishbourne rose to his not inconsiderable height, smoothing down his uniform over his trim, fit body before donning his gloves. "I ask nothing of you—your King asks nothing of you—save that you report any strangers to the area and any goings on that appear peculiar. You and the Earl are not to involve yourselves directly in any way, of course. I only felt it fair to warn you about the shore, so that neither of you is inadvertently taken as one of the Gentlemen by my men, who on occasion will be, with your kind permission, patrolling the area at night.''

''I would not think to take on the daunting project of trying to capture an entire band of smugglers, Lieutenant. But if, as you suggest, there could be a spy—or even spies—operating near Seashadow, it would be my duty to do my utmost to capture him—or them!''

''Miss Dalrymple,'' the Lieutenant reiterated, ''we have everything well in hand. Please, ma'am, do not involve yourself. If anything should happen to you because of my visit, I should never forgive myself. If you see anyone acting suspiciously, just have one of your servants summon me.''

Reluctantly nodding her agreement, Elly escorted the Lieutenant to the door, past Lily, who was making a great fuss out of dusting a gleaming brass candlestick as she watched the handsome tall, blonde officer.

Before the man could retrieve his hat from the table, the young girl had snatched it up, dusting it thoroughly before handing it to him with a smile and a wink. ''There you go, you lovely man,'' Lily cooed sweetly. ''Oh, you are a tall one, aren't you? Drop in any time,'' she added with a wink before Elly pointedly cleared her throat and the young girl scooted for the safety of the kitchens.

''She belonged to the late Earl,'' Elly explained, only to amend hastily, ''That is, she was a servant in the household when my brother and I came to Seashadow. She's been given her head too much, I daresay, and I have not as yet had time to instruct her in the proper behavior of staff.''

The Lieutenant shook his head. ''There's no need to explain, madam. I've heard the late Earl was a bit of a runabout, but I'm sure you and the current Earl will set it all to rights.'' He looked around the large foyer, his faded green eyes taking on a hint that could almost be termed envy. ''This is a lovely establishment. It would be a grievous sin to have it less than perfect.'' He brightened, smiling down at Elly. ''But if your brother the Earl is anything like his gracious sister, I'm sure there is no worry of Seashadow succumbing to the vagaries of poor husbandry.''

Knowing that her younger brother was at that moment in the west wing billiard room, blocking out a mural depicting the evolution of an apple from first juicy bite to bared core, Elly smiled enigmatically, allowing the Lieutenant to comfort himself with his own visions of the new Earl, and waved the man on his way.

Once the door was closed behind him, Elly stood staring sightlessly at the heavy crystal chandelier that hung over the flower arrangement atop the large round table in the middle of the spacious foyer. ''Smugglers and spies,'' she intoned gravely, her curiously slanted brown eyes narrowing. ''Carrying intelligence to Bonaparte so that he can kill more of our young men. Young men like my poor love, Robert—cut down before they've had a chance to live, to marry, to have sons.'' She raised her chin in determination. ''Well, they won't be doing it from Seashadow. Not if I have anything to say about it!''

ALASTAIR LOWELL stood lost in a pleasant daydream on the small hill, gazing across the rocks and sand toward his ancestral home, watching as the sun danced on the mellow pink brick and reflected against the mullioned windows.

Seashadow was particularly lovely in the spring of the year. It was almost as lovely as it was in the summer, or the fall, or the winter. "Face it, man, you're in danger of becoming dotty about the place. Being near to death—not to mention the weeks spent in friend Hugo's airless hovel—have given you a new appreciation for those things you have taken for granted much too long."

He turned toward the water, smiling indulgently as he watched Hugo at play on the shore, chasing a painted lady—one of the thousands of butterflies that spanned the Mediterranean to cross the Channel each spring and make landfall on the edge of Kent. Dear Hugo. Whatever would he have done without him?

"I would have been breakfast for some sea creature, that's what I would have done," he reminded himself, his grey eyes narrowed and taking on hints of polished steel. "I mustn't allow my joy in being alive to distract me from the reason behind that joy—my near murder."

He turned back toward Seashadow, rubbing a hand reflectively across his bearded chin. He still found it difficult to believe that a new Earl had been installed in his family home, a fact he had discovered during his first clandestine meeting with Billie Biggs—once that devoted woman had finished thoroughly dampening his shirtfront with tears of joy over his lucky escape from drowning. His eyes narrowed. "So now

I have a logical suspect. I hope you're enjoying yourself, Leslie Dalrymple, Earl of Hythe, eating my food and drinking my wine—for if Wiggins's and my plan goes well, you are very soon going to be booted out of my house and then hung up by your murdering neck!''

''Eeeeek!''

''Aaaarrgh!''

What a commotion! What a to-do! What high-pitched, unbridled hysteria!

''What in bloody hell? Hugo!'' It all happened so quickly that Alastair was taken off guard, his hand automatically moving to his waist, and the sword that wasn't there. All he had was his cane, and he raised the thing over his head menacingly, vowing to do his best with the tools at hand, for obviously there was murder taking place just out of sight along the beach.

Cursing under his breath, he began to run down the hill toward the shore, the shifting sands beneath his feet nearly bringing him to grief more than once before he cannoned into Hugo—who had been running toward him at full tilt—and was thrown violently backward against the ground, his wind knocked out of him, his senses rattled.

Air returned painfully to his starving lungs and he took it in in deep, hurtful gulps. There were several painted ladies hovering over him, swirling about in circles like bright yellow stars. No, they were stars, brilliant five-pointed objects that hurt his eyes. But that was impossible, for it was just past noon. There couldn't be any stars.

He shook his head, trying to clear it, slowly becoming aware of a shadow that had fallen over the land.

Hugo. The man's enormous head blocked out the sun, the butterflies, and the circling stars.

"Aaarrgh," Hugo moaned, his hamlike hands inspecting Alastair from head to foot for signs of damage.

Suddenly a parasol, built more for beauty than for combat, came crashing down on Hugo's back, once, twice, three times, before splintering into a mass of painted sticks, pink satin, and lace.

"Unhand that man, you brute!" a woman's raised voice demanded imperiously. "Isn't it enough that you accost helpless females—must you now compound your villainy by trying to pick this poor fellow's pockets? Away with you, you cad, or it will be much the worst for you!"

Alastair struggled to sit up, trying his best not to succumb to the near fit of hilarity brought on by both Hugo's frantic expression and the outrageousness of the unknown female's accusations. This proved extremely difficult, as Hugo, who was obviously thoroughly cowed, had buried his face against the Earl's chest, seeking sanctuary. "I say, Hugo, leave off, do, else you're going to crush the life out of me," Alastair pleaded, trying to push the man to one side.

"You—you know this brute?" the woman asked, dropping the ruined parasol onto the sand, clearly astonished. "I came upon him as I rounded the small cliff over there. I thought he was a smuggler going to...but *he* must actually have been afraid of *me*...which is above everything silly, for he is four times my size...and then I took him for a robber when he was only trying to help you? This is all most confusing. I don't understand."

"That makes the two of us a matched set, madam, for I am likewise confused," Alastair replied, prudently reaching for his cane before attempting to rise and get his first good look at the woman who had so daringly defended him against Hugo.

She was a young woman of medium height, slightly built in her rather spinsterish grey gown, her fair hair scraped back ruthlessly beneath her bonnet so that she looked, to his eyes, like drawings he'd seen of recently scalped colonials. Her huge brown eyes were curiously slanted—probably a result of her skin-stretching hairstyle. She looked, and acted, like somebody's keeper, and he immediately pitied her "keepee."

"When last I saw friend Hugo here, for that is his name," Alastair continued, "he was amusing himself chasing a painted lady."

"I beg your pardon," the female said crushingly. "I have not insulted you, sirrah! Just because I am on the beach without a chaperone is no reason to—"

Alastair hastened to correct her misinterpretation. "A painted lady is but another name for a butterfly, madam—the two-winged variety, that is," he said, rising to his knees as Hugo put a hand under each of his arms and hauled his master ungainly to his feet. "Ah, there we are, almost as good as new. Thank you, Hugo," he said, having been righted satisfactorily. "Now, perhaps we might try to make some sense out of these past few minutes."

"I knew that," the woman said in a small voice.

"You knew what?" he asked, bemused by the slight blush that had crept, unwanted, onto her cheeks.

"I knew about painted ladies—that is, about butterflies," she stammered, looking at him as if she had never seen a man up close before. "Are you sure you are quite all right? That was quite a blow you took." Her voice trailed off as a humanizing grin softened her features. "You—you must have bounced at least three times," she added, belatedly trying to disguise the grin with one gloved hand. "Oh, I'm sorry! I shouldn't see any levity in this, should I?"

Alastair made to push the kneeling, still-quavering Hugo—who reminded him of an elephant cowering in fear of a mouse—away from his leg. "Oh, I don't know, madam. If we can't discover the levity in this scene, I should think we are beyond redemption." He held out his hand. "I am John Bates, by the way."

She looked at his outstretched hand, then pointedly ignored it, all her starch back in her posture. "I am Elinor Dalrymple, sister of Leslie Dalrymple, Earl of Hythe—on whose lands you, Mr. Bates, are trespassing. May I ask your business at Seashadow?"

"Aargg, ummff, aaah!"

"Yes, yes, Hugo, I quite agree with you. I shall tell the lady. Don't excite yourself," Alastair soothed, patting the giant's head as he tried desperately to gather his thoughts, and control his anger. Who was this unlovely chit to dare ask his business upon his own land?

Why, the only reason she was still here rather than rotting in some damp jail—her and her miserable, conniving brother—was due to his charity in not demanding they be arrested the moment he'd first learned of their usurpation of his lands and title. No, he corrected himself, that wasn't quite true. It had been Geoffrey Wiggins's idea (conveyed in a hurried meeting between the two men) to continue the deception Alastair had first planned while still recuperating in Hugo's hovel—and the romance of the thing was fast losing its allure.

"You know what he's saying?" Elly asked, clearly surprised, as she peeped around Alastair to get a better look at Hugo.

"By and large, Miss Dalrymple, by and large. Hugo doesn't plague one with a lot of idle chitchat, having lost his tongue in some way too terrible to tell. However, if you should wish for him to show you the wound, I'm sure he would be delighted to satisfy your—"

"That won't be necessary," Elly cut in quickly. "But you—you understand him, poor fellow?"

"Now who are you calling a poor fellow, I wonder? But never mind. I shall answer your question the best I can. Yes, Hugo and I have, by way of his most articulate grunts and some acting out of intent, learned some basic communication. For instance, I am sure Hugo is devastated at having frightened you—nearly as devastated as he is by his fear of you. Please wave and smile to him, if you will. I should like for him to feel secure enough to leave go his death grip on my leg, for it is just regaining its strength from the wound it lately suffered on the Peninsula."

"You were on the Peninsula?" Elly asked, dutifully smiling and waving to Hugo before returning her gaze to Alastair. "I'm so sorry. I didn't know."

"And how should you, madam?" Alastair asked, intrigued by her quick about-face. She seemed almost caring. "Tell me, is your brother the Earl in residence? I wished to thank him for renting me the cottage, but all I have seen thus far, other than your delightful presence, of course, was a slightly vacuous-looking youth walking the beach earlier, collecting seaweed for only the good Lord knows what purpose.''

He watched as Miss Dalrymple blushed yet again, and had the uncomfortable feeling that he had just struck a nerve. ''That vacuous-looking youth, as you termed him, Mr. Bates'' —she shot at him in some heat— ''is the Earl of Hythe—and I should thank you to have the goodness to keep your boorish opinions to yourself.'' So saying, she turned on her heels, about to flounce off, he was sure, in high dudgeon.

She had taken only three steps when—again, as he was sure she would—she turned back, her slightly pointed chin thrust out, to exclaim, ''What do you mean, sir—you wish to thank my brother for the use of the cottage? What cottage? Where?''

As Hugo had been distracted by another gaily colored painted lady and was lumbering down the beach in pursuit of the gracefully gliding butterfly, Alastair felt free to spew the remainder of his lies just as he and Wiggins had practiced them. ''Why, madam, I thought you knew. After all, it was your brother who agreed to lend me the cottage on the estate while I recuperate from my wounds. It's the cottage just to the east of here—slightly inland, and with a lovely thatched roof. Hugo and I have been quite comfortable there for over a month now, although this is my first venture so far from my bed. But you still appear confused, Miss Dalrymple—and you shouldn't frown so, it will cause lines in your forehead.''

''Never mind my forehead, if you please!'' Elly shot back, bending down to retrieve her ruined parasol. ''Wait a minute!'' she said as she straightened. ''Over a month ago, you say? Why, that must have been the late Earl. Of course! You rented the cottage from the late Earl! That's why Leslie and I weren't aware of it.''

''The Earl is dead? I have been out of touch, haven't I?'' Alastair bowed deeply from the waist. ''My condolences on your loss, madam.''

''None are required, Mr. Bates,'' Elly answered distractedly, clearly still trying to absorb his news. ''I never knew the horrible man, I'm happy to say.''

Alastair longed to take Elinor Dalrymple's slim throat in his hands and crush the life out of her. Smiling through gritted teeth, he responded, ''Then may I offer my congratulations to your brother and yourself, for surely the two of you have fallen into one of the deepest gravy boats in all England. The late Earl was known, after all, for his great wealth.''

''That's not all the late Earl was known for,'' Elly said, sniffing. ''He was a profligate, useless drain on society, if half the stories I have heard are to be believed. If you wish to talk about painted ladies, you should have been here for his memorial service. There were more butterflies at Seashadow that day than this, if you take my meaning.''

This time Alastair could not suppress a grin. ''Lots of weeping and gnashing of teeth, was there? There's many a man who would relish such a send-off. Was there a redhead among them? I'd heard the late Earl had quite a ravishing redhead in keeping.''

Elly's spine stiffened once more, most probably, Alastair supposed, more in self-censure at her own loose tongue than at his daring response to her indiscreet chatter. ''Be that as it may be, if he leased a returning veteran a cottage in which to recuperate, he did at least one good deed in his wasted lifetime, and I shall not take this one vestige of goodness from his memory by refusing to honor his wishes.''

''You are kindness itself, Miss Dalrymple,'' Alastair cooed, longing to throttle her.

''The sea air will doubtless be salutary to your wounds,'' she continued. ''As a matter of fact—as a small way of showing you Seashadow's hospitality— may I tell my brother that you are to join us this evening for dinner?''

Alastair smiled, succeeding in splitting the three-week growth of beard so that his even white teeth sparkled in the sunlight. ''Madam,'' he said sincerely, ''I should be delighted!''

THE EVENING WAS comfortably cool, with a slight breeze coming off the sea as Elly stood just outside the French doors watching the sea birds as they circled the beach. Raising a hand to her throat, she adjusted the cameo that hung from a thin ivory ribbon, wondering if jewelry—even such simple jewelry—was proper during her supposed time of mourning for her cousin, the late Earl.

''Oh, pooh,'' she said, allowing her hand to drop to her side, where it found occupation smoothing the skirt of her silver-grey gown. ''What does it matter anyway, now that you've been so stupid as to express your true feelings about the man to a relative stranger—a relative stranger you have invited to dinner, and then dressed yourself up like some man-hungry spinster at her last prayers?''

She should have invited Lieutenant Fishbourne to join them as well, considering the fact that his warning to her was the main reason she had invited John Bates to dine. "Report any strangers to the area and any goings-on that appear peculiar," the Lieutenant had cautioned her, and Elly had every intention of reporting John Bates and Hugo to the Lieutenant just as soon as she was sure if they were smugglers or spies. She only needed to squeeze a bit more pertinent information from Mr. John Bates so that she wouldn't disgrace herself by turning in an innocent man.

"John Bates couldn't be innocent," she told herself reassuringly, hearing the brass door knocker bang loudly in the foyer, announcing her dinner guest's arrival. "Nobody that handsome—or forward—could possibly be innocent."

Stepping into the drawing room, she looked around to see that Leslie, who had been dutifully sitting in the blue satin striped chair when she had left the room, was nowhere to be found. "Leslie?" she hissed, looking about desperately as she heard footsteps approaching the room. "Leslie! You promised! Where are you?"

"Lose something?" a voice inquired from behind her just as she was peeking through the fronds of a towering fern in hopes of discovering her brother hiding behind it.

Straightening, Elly pasted on a deliberate smile and turned to greet her guest. "Lose something?" she repeated blankly. "Why, yes, I seem to have misplaced, *um*, my knitting. Mrs. Biggs, our housekeeper, appears to delight in hiding it from me."

"You don't knit, Elly. Never could, without making a botch of the thing."

Elly swung about, to see Leslie down on all fours

behind the settee. "Leslie!" she gritted under her breath. "Get up at once. What are you doing down there?"

Leslie Dalrymple, Earl of Hythe, rose clumsily to his feet, his pale blonde hair falling forward over his high forehead, his knees and hands dusty. "I was sitting quite nicely, just as you instructed, Elly, when a breeze from the doorway sent the loveliest dust bunny scurrying across the floor. See!" he demanded, holding up a greyish round ball of dust. "I think it's just the thing to complete my arrangement of Everyday Things, don't you?"

Elly didn't know whether to hit her brother or hug him. He looked so dear, standing there holding his dust bunny as if it were the greatest treasure on God's green earth, yet he was making the worst possible impression on John Bates. John Bates! Elly whirled to face her handsome guest, daring him with her eyes to say one word—one single, solitary word against her beloved brother.

Her fears, at least for the moment, proved groundless. John Bates, who had indeed witnessed all that had just transpired, only advanced across the width of the Aubusson carpet, his golden hair and beard glinting in the candlelight, his cane in his left hand as he favored his left leg, his right hand outstretched in greeting.

"My Lord Hythe, it is a distinct pleasure to meet you," he said, his tone earnest even to Elly's doubting ears. "I wish to thank you for agreeing to honor the rental arrangement made between the late Earl and myself. And, oh yes, please allow me to offer you condolences on your loss."

Leslie looked down on the dust bunny. "But I didn't lose it. See, I have it right here."

"Mr. Bates is referring to our libertine cousin Alastair's untimely death," Elly corrected sweetly even as she glared at John Bates. He already knew how she felt about her late cousin. Why was he persisting in bringing it up again and again? Anyone would think they had killed the stupid man, for pity's sake!

The dust bunny disappeared into Leslie's coat pocket as he took John's hand, wincing at the older man's firm grip. "A strong one, aren't you? Oh, you meant m'cousin, of course. Please excuse Elly. M'sister's taken a pet against him for some reason, ever since his mourners wouldn't stay to tea after the service, as a matter of fact. Rather poor sporting of her to my way of thinking, as the fellow's dead, ain't he—leaving the two of us as rich as Croesus into the bargain."

"Leslie, please," Elly begged quietly, steering the two men toward the settee and seating herself in the blue satin chair.

But Leslie was oblivious to his sister's pleading. Seating himself comfortably, one long, skinny leg crossed over the other, he informed his guest, "I have been considering composing a picture to honor the late Earl and his accomplishments—only, I can't seem to find that he actually accomplished anything, except a few things best not remembered. I'm an artist, you understand."

"You wish to do a portrait?" Alastair asked, to Elly's mind, a bit intensely.

Leslie waved his thin, artistic hands dismissingly. "No, no. Never a portrait. That's so mundane—so ordinary. No, I wish to execute a chronicle of Alastair's life, with symbols. For instance,'' he expanded, thrilled to have found a new audience for his ideas, ''if I were to do Henry the Eighth, I should include a bloody ax, a joint of meat, weeping angels, a view of the Tower—you understand?''

''What a unique concept, my lord,'' Alastair complimented, his eyes shifting so that he was looking straight at Elly, who shivered under his penetrating, assessing grey gaze.

What was he looking at? she wondered. And why did she have the uncomfortable feeling that John Bates could prove to be a very dangerous man?

CHAPTER TWO

HE WAS STARING at Elinor Dalrymple; he knew he was, but he couldn't help himself. Alastair had come to Seashadow to unmask the new Earl as his attacker. It had seemed so simple, so straight-forward—in a backhanded sort of way. But Leslie Dalrymple, bless his paper skull, wouldn't harm a fly—even if he knew how. Alastair wasn't so bent on revenge that he couldn't see that.

Unfortunately, he told himself as Mrs. Biggs called them to the dinner table, that left only the sister, Elinor, to take Leslie's place as suspect. Offering Elinor his arm to escort her in to dinner, and throwing a stern look at Mrs. Biggs, who so forgot herself as to begin a clumsy curtsey as he moved past (after she had done so well earlier when he had first arrived at the door), Alastair knew he had to rethink his deductions.

A man, after all, did not accuse another man of attempted murder without a wheelbarrow full of irrefutable evidence. Wasn't the desire to accumulate evidence what had brought him, under an assumed identity, to Seashadow in the first place? But a man—at least any man who considered himself to be a gentleman—never accused a lady of anything.

Once he had helped Elinor to her seat and taken his own chair across from her, Alastair resumed staring at her, knowing he was dangerously close to being indiscreet, but unable to help himself. A woman! It had never occurred to him that his attacker could be a woman. Oh, certainly she had employed someone to actually perform the dirty deed—to conk him on the head and send him to a watery grave—but that didn't make her any less guilty, did it?

This was going to take some getting used to, Alastair decided, deliberately smiling at Elinor Dalrymple, as if enchanted by her spinsterish charms and idly wondering if her small, shell-like ears really fit so snugly against the sides of her head or if her ruthlessly pulled-back hair had anything to do with it. He watched her spine straighten as it had on the beach and this time recognized the action as the proud, stiff-necked posture of one who has had more than a nodding acquaintance with poverty.

And with a brother like Leslie to support her, he considered thoughtfully, is it any wonder the two of them had been purse-pinched? He doubted he had to look much further for a motive.

"Do I have a smut on my nose?"

Alastair blinked, his attention caught by the question in Elinor's voice, although he hadn't quite comprehended what she had said, his attention still concentrated on her blonde hair as he tried to imagine her as she would look with it soft and loose against her high-cheeked face. "I beg your pardon?"

"You're staring, Mr. Bates," she pointed out needlessly. "I wondered if there was something wrong with me that has put you off your food. You haven't even touched your meal, and Big George has really outdone himself with the veal."

"Yes, indeed, I have—" Alastair had always relished Big George's way with veal—so much so that he nearly gave himself away, only catching himself in time to amend his conversation by ending, "always enjoyed a veal. Big George, you say? Is there also, perchance, a Little George running about somewhere?"

Leslie Dalrymple, his mouth full of veal, answered. "Little Georgie, actually, even though he's past eighteen and fully grown. He doesn't cook, though—big George won't let him, at least, according to Mrs. Biggs, not since he set the capons on fire. Little Georgie just helps. Biggs is their name. You already met Mrs. Biggs, our housekeeper. Big George is her husband."

"Making Little Georgie their son," Elinor completed hastily. "It is as logical as it is boring, Leslie, my dear, and before you launch into a dissertation on all the other little Biggses running tame about Seashadow, I suggest a change of subject. Perhaps our guest would rather discuss something more worldly than our servant situation." Leaning forward slightly, she went on encouragingly, "You served with Wellington perhaps, Mr. Bates? What battles were you in, exactly—and *when?*"

Alastair was amazed at the obvious intensity of her interest. He suddenly felt like a prisoner in the dock, undergoing a detailed cross-examination bent on exposing his guilt in some heinous crime. "Well, actually, madam, I didn't see much action before—"

Leslie stuck out his bottom lip petulantly and interrupted, "Who cares, Elly? I wanted to tell Mr. Bates about Rosie.'' He brightened slightly, looking to his sister. ''I'm going to paint her, you know.''

''Yes, dearest, I do know,'' Elinor said, reaching over to pat her brother's hand. ''Rosie will be a wonderful subject, once she cuts her second teeth. Now, why don't you try some of those lovely peas?''

Alastair watched, bemused, as Leslie obediently picked up his fork and began to eat. Oh yes, there was no question as to just who was in charge here. Elinor Dalrymple of the flat ears, scraped-back hair, and miserable disposition—sitting at her brother's right hand—was the real Earl of Hythe in all but name. Wait until he ran this one past Wiggins!

''Mr. Bates?''

Alastair looked across the table at Elinor, his grey eyes deliberately wide, his expression purposely guileless. If he had decided nothing else, he had decided that this woman was intelligent—which also made her dangerous. ''Yes, Miss Dalrymple?''

''You were telling us about your time with Wellington,'' she prompted, accepting a small serving of candied yams from the hovering Mrs. Biggs. ''From the left, Mrs. Biggs. You serve from the left.''

''Do yer wants 'em or not, missy?'' Mrs. Biggs challenged, glaring at Alastair as if begging his permission to dump the bowl on Elinor's head. ''Right, left. What does it matter? I've got Baby Willie crying in the kitchen, afraid of that horsey-faced brute, Hugo, and that lazy, good-for-nothin' Lily nowheres ter be found.''

''Baby Willie's crying?'' Leslie exclaimed, hopping from his seat so quickly, the chair nearly toppled behind him. ''We can't have that, Elly, now can we?''

He reached up to pull the large linen serviette from his shirt collar, where he had obediently tucked it after dripping soup on his neckcloth. "I know. I'll make him a crow from this serviette—of course, it will be white rather than black, but then, that just adds to the romance of the thing, doesn't it? I can use these peas for eyes," he went on excitedly, filling his hand with the green vegetable before heading for the kitchens. "It will be famous, I vow it will! Here I come, Baby Willie! *Caw! Caw!*"

"Leslie, come back here—" Elinor began as Alastair hid a grin behind his own serviette. "Oh, what's the use? It's like speaking to the wind."

His sense of the ridiculous overcoming his good manners, Alastair threw back his head and laughed aloud for a moment before sobering and apologizing almost meekly, "I'm sorry, Miss Dalrymple. I am but a lowly soldier sitting at an Earl's table. I really shall have to cultivate more elegance of mind. But you have to own it, Miss Dalrymple—your brother is most amusing."

Her brown eyes turned as black and forbidding as an angry sea. "You think he's an utter addlepate, don't you, Mr. Bates?" she accused hotly. "Well, perhaps he is, but Leslie is my addlepate, and I'll thank you to keep your thoughts to yourself!"

Alastair waved his hands in front of his face, as if to ward off her accusations. "No, no, Miss Dalrymple, please don't fly into the treetops. I meant nothing by it, really I didn't. Besides, you are wrong. Your brother is not an addlepate. He's rich, madam, which makes him a delightful eccentric. Only a poor man is an addlepate."

There was a commotion in the kitchens that reached into the dining room, turning the heads of both its occupants toward the baize door just as Hugo exploded into the room, Leslie on his arm. "Elly, look! A giant. A Titan! Isn't it above everything famous!"

Leslie turned delighted eyes to Alastair, who felt himself rapidly wilting beneath Elinor's white-hot glare. He had brought Hugo along with him because he couldn't feel right leaving him alone in the cottage. He'd had no idea the man's presence would cause either Baby Willie's tears or Leslie's euphoria.

"Is he really yours?" Leslie went on in accents of rapture. "Mrs. Biggs says he is. Do you think I could borrow him? I've just had the happy notion of painting him—for comparison, you understand—alongside of Baby Willie, if that poor dear will ever stop crying. Hugo's the loveliest thing I've ever seen!"

"*Aaahh,*" Hugo crooned softly, accepting the compliment most graciously by picking Leslie up by the coat collar with one hand and placing a smacking wet kiss on his lordship's thin cheek.

Elinor leapt to her feet. "You brute! You put my brother down this instant!"

"*Aaarrrggh!*"

Feeling as if he had just stepped unawares into a Covent Garden farce, Alastair rose as well, ordering, "Don't growl, Hugo. It isn't polite. And put his lordship down; I think he's having a spot of trouble getting his breath."

"Dear me!" Leslie gulped, nervously smoothing his neckcloth as he gazed up at the giant. "He is a strong fellow, isn't he? But not to worry, Elly, I'm convinced that Hugo and I will become fast friends. Won't we, Hugo?''

The giant grinned, showing the gap between his teeth—the sight of which immediately transported Leslie into another bout of ecstasy—and gently patted the young man's blonde head. "Glugg, glugg," he crooned affectionately.

"That is *it!*" Elinor exclaimed, the high pitch of her voice clearly indicating that she was about to fly into the boughs. Alastair privately commended her restraint, for he should surely have exploded long ago had he been so pressed. "Leslie, excuse yourself," she ordered in a voice that brooked no opposition, and her brother meekly left the room, turning only once, to wave goodbye to Hugo.

She then turned to Alastair and said coldly, "Mr. Bates, as you are living on the estate, we shall doubtless be forced to deal with each other from time to time—at least until I can have my brother's solicitor make other arrangements for you. But for the moment, sir, I ask nothing from you other than that you retrieve your cane, whistle this brute to heel, and remove yourself from these premises at once!"

Alastair, who had grown heartily sick of Hugo's attempts at the culinary arts over the past weeks, eyed the veal hungrily before giving in to the inevitable. The evening had been a shambles from odd beginning to even odder end. But, knowing that tomorrow was another day, he wisely motioned to Hugo, and the two of them headed for the door.

They had just stepped onto the porch—the heavy oak door slamming behind them, obviously propelled by the gentle hand of their hostess—when an insistent *"psst, psst"* came from the bushes.

"Who's there?" Alastair whispered, looking about in the darkness as Hugo growled deep in his chest.

The bushes rustled behind them, and out stepped Lily Biggs, her hips undulating wildly as she approached, as if she were trying to navigate her way across a mound of feather pillows. "G'evenin', yer lordship," she crooned, batting her eyelashes at her master. "Mum told me yer was back, but I didn't believe it. She says I'm not ter say nuthin' about knowin' yer neither, or else I'll get my backside switched."

"Your mother is a very wise woman, Lily," Alastair said, idly inspecting the impressive cleavage revealed by the snug white peasant blouse and wondering just when it was that the once angular young girl had developed the soft, enticing body of a woman. Had it really been that long since he'd visited his smallest, yet favorite, estate? "You won't betray me, will you, my little darling?"

With a toss of her head, Lily's long, dark hair resettled itself on her snowy white shoulders as she stood toe to toe with Alastair, her firm young breasts pressed invitingly against his chest. Reaching up with both hands to smooth his neckcloth, she grinned and purred, "And what would be in it fer little Lily, d'yer suppose, iffen she was ter do as yer says? I love yer beard, yer lordship," she continued, lightly stroking his face. "It's so golden—like the sun or somethin'— and so fuzzy."

Now, here was a dilemma to tax the brain of the wise Solomon himself. Alastair had been without a willing woman for more than a month—quite possibly a new personal record he wouldn't wish bruited about among his acquaintances. It would be nice having an unattached, willing female so close to hand—although he supposed he could just as easily import one from the city if he so wished.

Besides, Alastair had known this child since her birth, and would never do anything to betray Billie Biggs's faith in him. But at the same time—could he trust this willful child to keep his secret if he insulted her by turning down what she was so obviously offering?

"Lily, I—" he began at last, not really knowing what he was going to say, just as the oak door swung open in a rush and he looked toward it, praying it was Mrs. Biggs come to his rescue.

But, alas, just as it had been with the veal he'd hoped to enjoy, he wasn't going to be that lucky.

"Here, Mr. Bates, you forgot your—oh, good Lord!" Elinor exclaimed, her arm halting in the action of tossing Alastair's curly-brimmed beaver at him. "Oh, this is beyond anything low!" The beaver came winging toward him, to be deftly snatched out of the air by Hugo, who then sat the undersized thing atop his own oversized head. "You lech! Let go of that poor, innocent girl this instant!"

"Miss Dalrymple," Alastair began hastily, silently cursing his continuing run of bad luck, "this isn't what you think. Let me endeavour to explain."

He turned toward the doorway, slapping Lily's greedy hands away as he tried to explain. "Leave go, Lily, for God's sake," he hissed angrily. "Don't make this any worse than it is." He looked up into his hostess's angry face. "Miss Dalrymple—please listen to me!"

"Listen to you? Listen to you!" Elinor exploded, grabbing hold of Lily's elbow and yanking her up the steps and into the foyer. "I have two eyes, don't I, Mr. Bates? There is nothing you can say that could possibly erase the evidence my own eyes have delivered. You may be a veteran, but you are no gentleman. Kindly keep to your cottage until I speak to my brother's solicitor—and don't try to approach this house or any of its inhabitants again. Do you hear me?"

"I should think they heard you in Dover, madam," Alastair replied tightly, his pride stung. "And once again, Miss Dalrymple, I bid you good night. It has truly been an experience." Feeling he had gotten in the last word, he then limped off into the night, Hugo, as Elinor Dalrymple had so imperiously ordered, at his heels.

"HERE THEY COME! I can see the bow of the boat hitting against the waves, turning them white. They're about to land."

"Quietly, your lordship, quietly," Captain Geoffrey Wiggins admonished in a fierce whisper. "There are three of us and twenty-five of them. I don't much like the odds."

Alastair pushed his prone frame more closely against the body-sized hollow he had dug in the sand, kicking out his left foot as some hungry insect feasted on his ankle bone.

"Then why in bloody hell didn't you bring more men? You told me you were almost certain the Gentlemen were landing here tonight. If I had known when you came to my cottage that all you wanted was for me to put lampblack all over my face and hands and burrow in the sand and watch, I could have stayed by my fire, dreaming about the veal I didn't get to eat while trying to down Hugo's swill—no offense, Hugo," he shot back over his shoulder to where Hugo was likewise lying half-buried in the sand. "What an evening I have had! I tell you, Geoffrey, the Dalrymple woman is mean; mean clear through to the bone."

"Shhhh!" Wiggins hissed, trying his best to bury his short, round body deeper in the sand. The Gentlemen were on the shore below them now, hastily unloading their cargo of brandy kegs, each gang member hoisting a barrel onto his shoulders before heading inland, the boat returning to the sea. "Count them," he whispered imperiously.

"Christ on a crutch, man," Alastair gritted back at him in exasperation, still itching to do combat with something other than the insects that continued to plague them, "you can bloody well count them yourself! What do I look like, a schoolboy at his sums?"

But, his protestations to one side, he did as the older man bid, dutifully counting kegs and gang members until the last of them trailed away over the hill to whatever hidey-hole they had chosen to stash their booty until it could be dispatched farther inland.

"It's just as I had thought, your lordship," Captain Wiggins said at last in quiet satisfaction, clambering to his feet and wiping his sandy palms briskly against each other.

"Don't look so pleased with yourself, Wiggins, or I might just do you an injury. Just as you thought about what?'' Alastair asked, turning over so that he could prop his sitting form against an outcrop of rock, his filthy hands dangling from atop his propped-up knees. "This may come as something of a shock to you, old man, but it wasn't what I thought at all. We came, we saw, we did nothing. No wonder you fellows at the War Office asked for my help. I'm bloody surprised old Boney ain't tripping down the dance at Almack's with Silence Jersey on his arm, nattering at him nineteen to the dozen, if this is the way you go about things. Hugo, stop threatening Captain Wiggins! I'll fight my own battles, thank you.''

The usually gentle giant, who had been eyeing Geoffrey Wiggins in a menacing way that had the squat, rotund man looking about himself as if planning a hasty retreat, growled low in his throat and moved off into the darkness.

Alastair waved Hugo on his way, his teeth flashing white in the faint light of the approaching dawn as he smiled at Wiggins's obvious relief. "And you worried about my safety, Wiggins,'' he said, shaking his head. "I hope your mind is set at ease now.''

"In all my fifty years, your lordship,'' the Captain said, extracting a huge red handkerchief to wipe his sweaty brow, "I have never seen the like. How big is he, anyway?''

"Seven feet? Twenty-five stone? He is slightly smaller than Westminster Abbey, however,'' Alastair answered disinterestedly, rising so that he looked down at the older man, his hands on his hips. "Now, if we are done discussing the so estimable Hugo's dimensions, perhaps you can explain why we have partaken in this ridiculous, uncomfortable exercise.''

"Ridiculous? How so, sir?"

Alastair shook his head in disgust at the question. "You came to my cottage at midnight—throwing those pebbles against the window was a tad dramatic, Geoffrey, by the by—promising me a sight of the smugglers you commissioned me to help ferret out for you. I'll say one thing for you—you didn't promise more than you delivered. We did see them, for all the sense it made. All we did was lie in the sand for three hours—I've been bitten badly, fleas I suppose—while we watched them land at Seashadow, and then counted them as they passed us. I could just as easily have taken your word for it, you know, and remained happily at home."

Wiggins shook his head, his bushy grey side-whiskers serving as anchors as his chubby cheeks swung back and forth. "Didn't you see, your lordship? There were twenty-five smugglers, and only twenty-four casks! Think, your lordship!"

Alastair shrugged, not comprehending. "So? One of them is a lazy bugger. What of it?"

"Think again, please, sir. The Gentlemen never waste a motion. One of them," the Captain imparted importantly, "wasn't a smuggler!"

The dawn broke, both literally and figuratively, as Lord Hythe snapped his fingers. "A spy?"

Wiggins nodded emphatically. "Precisely, my lord, very good. And I got a fairly good look at his face. I'm sure I'll recognize him when I see him again—as I can promise you I will. The brandy casks were only a diversion, probably a gift to the men who helped him cross the Channel. A truly dedicated group of the Gentlemen would have brought twice the booty—and no passengers. Twenty-four casks weren't worth the trouble of trying to get past Lieutenant Fishbourne and his men. Oh, yes, your lordship, we have found our man at long last!''

Alastair brightened even more. This was good news. ''Then there is no need to continue this masquerade! Actually you never needed me at all, Wiggins, now that I think on it, although I do appreciate that you thought to include me. I only wish I could have discovered all this myself, but I was conked on the head and thrown overboard before I could do more than plan my first moves against the men you thought were using Seashadow's beaches. Now it will be a simple matter of surrounding the beach with soldiers and apprehending the fellow. When do you think he'll be back? I'd like to be here, of course.''

The Captain sighed. This was the most difficult part of his job—dealing with civilians. War Office matters were best left to those in the service, those who understood tactics, maneuvers—the workings of the enemy mind. It certainly hadn't been Geoffrey Wiggins's idea to bring the Earl of Hythe in on this enterprise. ''Thy will be done,'' the Captain blasphemed, raising his eyes to the heavens and seeing his desk-bound, hide-bound superior in the War Office. He sighed again.

Alastair Lowell may have been young, and relatively inexperienced, but he knew when he had leapt to an incorrect conclusion. ''He's just a little fish, isn't he, Wiggins? You're after bigger fish.''

The Captain looked at the Earl with growing respect. ''Precisely, your lordship! The man we just saw is but a paid courier. I have men waiting along the roadway, ready to follow him to his final destination. We want to know who he is reporting to in London. We brought you into the exercise, your lordship, because we wished permission to operate freely from Seashadow, as we were convinced that the courier was using your portion of the coast. But then, when the attempt came on your life so soon after we had spoken to you, we feared that our plan to spring our trap had been found out.''

''But, as I keep telling you, Wiggins, I'm convinced that the attempt had nothing whatever to do with spies or espionage. It couldn't have done. Why, you had only told me about your suspicions a week earlier and I hadn't so much as lifted a finger to do anything more than give you permission to set yourself up as John Bates in the cottage I'm living in now. It's a good thing you hadn't as yet introduced yourself around the area, so that everyone believes me to be you. No,'' he concluded, his eyes narrowing as he conjured up a vision of Elinor as she had stood at his front door accusing him of lechery, ''it's that miserable Dalrymple woman, Wiggins. She's the one behind the attempt on my life! All that remains is to figure out whether she did it for love of her brother or love of money.''

''Be that as it may be, your lordship,'' Wiggins said resignedly, ''I still think I should inform Lieutenant Fishbourne that you are one of us. He is, after all, in charge of this area, and as hot to catch himself a clutch of smugglers and spies as any man I have ever met. Very dedicated, Lieutenant Fishbourne is, as well as eagerly looking out for a chance to improve his standing with his superiors. I have to return to London in at least a fortnight, you understand, to set things in motion from that end, and it wouldn't do to have the good Lieutenant arresting you on suspicion of being the man we're after while I'm not here to identify you, now would it, sir?''

Alastair shook his head at this argument, which he had heard before from the Captain. ''We'll allow Lieutenant Fishbourne to continue in his ignorance, Wiggins. But don't worry, I'll handle him if it becomes necessary. Remember, I was almost killed. Somebody wants me dead. If you are right, and the Dalrymple woman is innocent—well, I simply don't know who my friends are right now, Wiggins, and it is an uncomfortable feeling. I don't mean to set your back up with my stubbornness, but I'm chary of confiding in anyone just now. Frankly, if it hadn't been that I needed the cottage to lend credence to the story we conjured up between us, even you still wouldn't know that the real Earl of Hythe is alive.''

''GOOD AFTERNOON to you, my lord, madam.''

Elly stiffened, the lilt of good humor in John Bates's cultured voice cutting through her like a dull knife, and turned to face him as he carefully made his way down the incline onto the beach, his cane in his right hand.

Wait a moment! His right hand? She closed her eyes, trying to remember how he'd looked as he'd crossed the drawing room to greet her and Leslie the previous evening.

He'd looked handsome, and as dangerous as the devil, that she remembered clearly, although she kept telling herself to banish such debilitating thoughts from her mind. And he'd had the cane in his left hand as he favored his left leg. She was sure of it.

But this afternoon—ah, this afternoon—he was favoring his *right* leg. Wait until she told Lieutenant Fishbourne about this! If the Lieutenant wanted a spy, she couldn't think of a better candidate than the insufferable John Bates. But first she would have to be sure, and to be sure she would have to force herself to suffer the man's company at least one more time.

"Good afternoon to you, sir," she said with a forced air of cheerfulness, considering it safer to humor the man by pretending to forgive his boorishness of the previous evening until he could be clapped in irons. "Please allow me to apologize for my wretched behavior last evening. Mrs. Biggs graciously reminded me of Lily's predisposition to throwing herself at anything in—that is, I was made to understand that I was mistaken to blame you for Lily's, *um,* for Lily's—"

"Apology accepted, Miss Dalrymple, and the incident already forgotten," Alastair cut in, rescuing her from further embarrassment with his easy forgiveness while not sounding in the least penitent for his own misbehavior—and making her twice as angry with him as she had been the night before.

How dare he be so nice, so condescending, so easy to placate? She had thrown the man out of the house, then all but accused him of immorality, for heaven's sake! Didn't he have any pride, any feelings of self-worth? The man should be outraged!

The fact that he wasn't—or at least was pretending that he wasn't—was only further proof that he had some special, undoubtedly nefarious reason to want to stay at Seashadow.

Swallowing down hard on her anger, Elly simpered (oh, yes, she knew she was simpering, but she was doing it, after all, for King and country), "How kind of you, Mr. Bates. Might I call you John, I wonder? We are to be neighbors, after all, aren't we?"

"And you are kindness and charity itself, Miss Dalrymple," he responded, bowing deeply—most probably, Elly assumed meanly, to hide his triumphant smile at her veiled admission that she was not about to throw him out of the cottage as she had threatened. This entire stilted exchange, she knew, was as if the two of them were performing some intricate dance, with each of them being extremely careful about not treading on the other's toes.

Leslie, who had been silent all this time, now piped up cheerfully, while simultaneously showing his main concern in the matter, "Oh, good! I made a sad hash of my first social engagement as Earl—or so Elly told me at great length this morning—but everything seems to be settled most happily now." He turned to his sister, tugging on her arm like a small child begging for a treat. "Elly, does this mean I shall be able to have Hugo pose for me after all? I have had the most splendid idea of painting his massive hands as they gently cradle a purple butterfly."

"But, my lord, I believe the painted ladies are white, and yellow, and even black," John corrected pleasantly.

"Not to Leslie's eyes, John," Elly informed him, her tone daring him to laugh. "Leslie sees things differently with his artist's eyes."

"Precisely! Deep, pulsating purple—for the pulsating blue blood of royalty. The royal butterfly, gaudy and fragile, nestled in the strength of the great, callused hands of the masses.'' Leslie grabbed hold of Hugo's elbow. "You understand, Hugo, don't you? You, my friend, are to represent all of loyal England. It's quite an honor, you know.''

"Indeed, yes,'' John agreed in earnest tones, earning himself a cutting look from Elinor, which he returned with a smile and a wink.

Leslie remained oblivious to the none-too-subtle undercurrents of animosity swirling about him. "John,'' he piped up brightly, "I'll tell you what. I should really like to study Hugo some more before I paint him. Do you think we cold take a walk, spend a pleasurable hour as I come to know his many faces, his many moods? But before you answer, I must warn you, John. If you say no, I am not sure I can regard it. I am set on this. The apple was beginning to bore me to distraction—not to mention the flies it was drawing.''

"The apple?'' John whispered in an amused aside to Elly as he smiled and nodded his approval of Leslie's scheme. "Or would it be better if I didn't ask?''

"It would be immensely better if you didn't ask,'' she told him quietly, wondering why she suddenly felt as if, at last, there was someone in her life with whom she might be able to talk without feeling she had been dropped feet first into Bedlam. How terrible it was that the man she felt she could talk with was a Bonapartist spy!

Leslie, not noticing the quiet exchange—as he noticed less than nothing if it did not involve him directly—took up Hugo's hand and began walking toward Seashadow, only to stop some twenty feet

distant, whirl about, and call out loudly: "Did I bid
you good day, John? I sometimes forget to do that—
saying hallo and good day. Elly hates that, and I
wouldn't want to put her in one of her pets."

"I don't have pets!" Elly growled softly as John's
shoulders began to shake in obvious mirth. "I have
only been trying to put it across to him that he
shouldn't be surprised if he doesn't get along in society if he just walks away from people without saying
goodbye—just because he's been struck by some
grand, artistic inspiration."

"It's just that she says people in society won't like
an Earl who doesn't say goodbye," Leslie shouted
across the sand, confirming Elly's explanation. "Not
that I should care for all the toing and froing of Polite
Society. I like it here, actually, much more than half.
Well, toodle-oo, John. I'll bring him back—I promise!"

Elly put a hand to her head and sighed.

"You have the headache now, I suppose," she
heard John suggest, his words penetrating the dense
fog of her embarrassment.

Looking up to see the amusement in his face, she
heard herself reply, "You must think you have a most
winning smile behind that horrid beard, as you grin all
the time. Much as I wish not to do fatal damage to
your sensibilities, John, I think you look quite terrible."

The moment the words were out, Elly regretted
them. How was she supposed to get close to this
man—this miserable Bonapartist spy—if she persisted
in saying such horrid things? She was so enraged with
herself that she just stood there, staring up at him,

unable to think of a single thing to say that would heal their most recent breach.

But she shouldn't have worried. She should have known that John Bates's skin was too thick to be penetrated by her feeble female insults. Slipping her unprotesting hand through his elbow, he merely began walking them down the beach, in the opposite direction from that taken by Leslie and Hugo.

"Mad as fire, aren't you?" he said as calmly as if he were making everyday conversation. "Ah, madam, you have cut me to the quick. And here I had dared to dream that we were beginning to get on almost civilly. But there you are. Tell me, Miss Dalrymple. Are you aware that we are without a chaperone?"

CHAPTER THREE

SHE WAS BLUSHING. Good Lord above, she was blushing—just as if she were some silly, simpering miss
lately escaped from the schoolroom! It was mortify-
ing! How dare he bring such a lapse to her attention—
and grin through those horrid golden whiskers as he
did it? She should slap him silly, that's what she
should do.

No! She should pull her hand from its strangely
comfortable resting place through the crook of his elbow, turn on her heels, and march posthaste back to
Seashadow, cutting him dead.

No! She should face him down, stab him with her
cold, steely stare, then proceed to slice a few wide,
painful strips off his splendidly put-together hide with
a few well-chosen words meant to depress his absurd
familiarity once and for all.

No! She should take his cane (as it was obviously
useless to his two perfectly healthy legs) and hit him
repeatedly over the—

"Cat got your tongue, Miss Dalrymple? I was only
teasing, you know. After all, it's the middle of the
afternoon, your brother the Earl is just down the beach,
and we're in full sight of Seashadow. It isn't as if we
are about to elope together to Gretna Green, is it?"

Oh, how she hated—how she *loathed*—this insuf-

ferable man! Why didn't he just come out and say it—
she was an over-the-hill spinster who should have long
since donned her caps and stopped embarrassing
everyone by pretending she was still an eligible *parti*.
She couldn't cause a scandal if she were alone with
any man in the kingdom—save perhaps Prinny himself, who was known to like his women a little longer
in the tooth.

"Miss Dalrymple?" John Bates stopped walking to
step in front of her, tuck his cane under his arm, and
take hold of both her elbows as he stared down into
her face. "Oh, dear. I have put my foot in it, haven't
I? Both feet, perhaps. You're thinking that I'm thinking that you are ugly or something—aren't you? I assure you, Miss Dalrymple, that thought never entered
my head."

Elly finally found her voice. She didn't give a tin-
ker's dam if he were King of the Smugglers, Emperor
of the Spies, or both. She had had enough! "I think,
Mr. Bates, you do protest too much. For an idea that
never entered your head, it certainly found its way out
of your mouth quickly enough. Now, please unhand
me. I wish to return to my brother."

She made to withdraw herself from his hold, but he
thwarted her, his hands clamping down onto her
wrists. "Bristly as a prickly pear, aren't you, Miss
Dalrymple? I imagine I shall have to own it—I have
had occasion to consider your looks over the past few
days." He tipped his head this way and that, as if
giving her one last inspection before rendering his decision. "It's your hair, I think. I mean, your face is
unexceptional—a bit finely drawn perhaps, with a hint
of a pointed chin, and your strangely slanted brown

eyes are by far your best, most entrancing feature—
but your hair, Miss Dalrymple, is a disaster.''

"Oh, that's *it!*" Elly shouted in exasperation, feeling as if she were about to become totally unhinged.
She yanked herself free of his hands. "I may be destined to lead apes in hell through all eternity, Mr.
Bates, but I see no reason I should *listen* to one of
them babble while I'm still above ground."

She set off up the beach as fast as her jean half
boots, her swirling muslin skirts, and the shifting sands
allowed, knowing without seeing that he was close at
her heels, his limp forgotten.

"But, Miss Dalrymple, you didn't let me finish.
You have lovely hair—much the same color as mine,
as a matter of fact. Isn't that a coincidence? But you
yank it up on the top of your head like some tight-
lipped schoolmistress about to deliver a stern lecture."

Elly stopped in her tracks. Just as he had hit her
sore spot, her looks, he had just as unerringly struck
her one soft spot—her hair. She had lovely hair? She
had always thought so, privately, and could admit to
herself that she spent more hours in front of her mirror
brushing the heavy, waist-length locks than was absolutely necessary.

Once, she had worn it down. Once, she had brushed
it over the curling stick and looped it gracefully atop
her head, allowing it to wave softly at the sides of her
face. Her fiancé, Robert, had always liked it best that
way, saying it reminded him of molten gold mixed
with silver. But once Robert had been lost to her, there
had been no reason, no inclination, to fuss with her
hair other than in the privacy of her chamber, away

from the eyes of the world. Her bottom lip began to quiver.

"Miss Dalrymple?" John questioned, stepping in front of her. "Oh, blast it all, you're crying, aren't you? I've made you cry. I always did have a tongue that was hinged at both ends—and the horrible habit of speaking before thinking." He took her hands in his, squeezing her fingers comfortingly. "Please, Miss Dalrymple, forgive me. I'm the scum of the earth, I'm the lowest of the low."

Elly heard the self-condemnation in his tone. It was entirely believable. She also saw the sympathy in his grey eyes. It was the sympathy that stiffened her lip and brought her back to reality. She had always hated sympathy. It was so useless, almost as useless as her overreaction to his observations.

She had more important things to consider. John Bates *was* the lowest of the low, with the tact and manners of a mediocre dandy. That shouldn't have surprised her, because John Bates was, she was sure, also a smuggler—or a spy.

Either way, he was a dastardly creature, the sort of slimy, money-mad, disloyal cad Lieutenant Fishbourne had talked about, who sacrificed fine British lives like Robert Talmadge's for his own profit—and she was going to unmask him and see him punished for his crimes, if she had to put up with his crudity and insults every time they met.

But, if she was really set on her plan—and she knew deep in her heart of hearts that she was—*she* too was going to have to somehow develop a thicker skin. Considering their encounters to date, that skin, she supposed quietly, would also have to boast the repelling characteristics of battle-quality steel mesh.

"You're forgiven, Mr. Bates—John," she said at last, trying her best not to smile as he heaved a sigh of relief. Obviously it was important to his dastardly plans for him to remain in the cottage on the estate. "You have said nothing I have not heard before from Leslie. He compares the styling of my hair to that of a yellow onion. But, your apology rendered and accepted, John—do you think you could be so good as to once again allow me the use of my hands? I have decided to give in to impulse and take down my hair. This isn't London, after all, and I have been harboring the urge to wear it loose just once, to blow free in the breeze from the Channel. It's a silly notion, I must say, but one I should wish to indulge in just this single time. Do you mind?"

Her heart pounding, Elly raised her hands to the top of her head and removed the pins that held her hair in a tight bun. It was the touch of his hands on hers, of all things, that had decided her once and for all that she was obligated to forge ahead for King and country; the touch of his hands and her thought that he reminded her of a lower-class London dandy.

There were, she had discovered, absolutely *no* calluses on his palms! Leslie had spoken of the callused hands of the workers of England. Surely soldiers would similarly have hard workman's hands—Lieutenant Fishbourne did.

Yet John Bates had the smooth, well-groomed hands and nails of a London dandy—not that she had ever been to London herself, but she was sure those effete, pompous nodcocks used more creams on their hands than any beauty-proud debutante or aging matron.

If she was going to get to the bottom of this—if she was going to find any evidence concrete enough to take to Lieutenant Fishbourne—she would have to become close enough to John Bates, trusted enough by John Bates, that he allowed her inside his cottage, where she could discover the truth about him.

And in order to do that, she would have to first capture the man's interest.

WHAT IN BLOODY HELL was the absurd woman doing now? Alastair hadn't been this nonplussed since, since—why, he couldn't remember a single time in his life when he had been at such a total loss for words, for coherent thought. Standing there dumbly, as if he had been momentarily converted into marble, he watched as Elinor Dalrymple—thin, over-the-hill, pointy-chinned, stick-in-the-sand, possible attempted murderess Elinor Dalrymple—stuffed hairpin after hairpin into her skirt pocket, while using her other hand to hold on to the tight yellow twist of hair.

When the last of the pins was disposed of, she bowed her head so that her face was hidden from him, scrubbed at her freed hair with her fingers, and then flung her head back so that a river of silver and gold flowed from her forehead to her narrow waist.

And then—directly in front of his eyes, like a lowly caterpillar shedding its cocoon—Elinor Dalrymple metamorphosed into the most glorious painted lady Alastair Lowell had ever been privileged to see!

Her smooth cheeks flushed a becoming pink with exertion—could any of that lovely color have come from the knowledge that she was facing a man whose mouth was at half cock?—Elinor's features changed from pinched to petite, finely sculpted by the hand of a master. Her brown eyes danced with delicious mischief. Her hair, that unbelievable, unexpected curtain of glory, seemed to have taken on a life of its own, and he immediately longed to run his fingers through it, bury his face in it, wrap his naked skin in its warm fire.

Alastair could feel his body responding to the stimuli of Elly's appearance, to the sweet violet scent of her hair as it billowed in the breeze off the Channel, to the moist sweetness of her mouth as she smiled up at him with all the guileless invitation of a first-time strumpet.

Oh, yes, Alastair told himself, holding on to his composure with every ounce of will he could muster, he most certainly would have to rethink importing a woman from London, although his sudden aversion to redheaded women worried him more than he'd care to admit at this moment.

Her hands on her hips, her entire stance daring him to speak, he heard her say, "Ah, you cannot imagine how I have been longing to do that. Well, John, do you still believe we are in no need of a chaperone?"

The little tart! She was baiting him, deliberately urging him to commit an action that—if the woman in question was, at least as far as the world knew, the sister of an Earl—could be seen as nothing less than a marriage-mandatory compromise of her reputation. He'd like to slap her silly. He'd like to grab her by the shoulders and—and kiss her until she begged for mercy!

Good God, what was he thinking? Only a month earlier this woman had tried to have him murdered! If nothing else convinced him of that, her actions of the last few minutes had shown him that Elinor Dalrymple might have been trying to present herself as a little mouse, a loving sister, a drab nonentity of no importance—but her *real* self was quite a different matter.

A few subtle insults directed at her lack of beauty had been pointed enough to scratch off the dowdy exterior and reveal the real woman inside. He could see that she was champing at the bit to have the official year of mourning over so that she could go to London and take it by storm—probably leaving her paper-witted brother, Leslie, behind at Seashadow to paint the Biggs's children in all their "moods." The cold-hearted harridan!

These thoughts flew through Alastair's mind like lightning bolts exploding against the unwary earth at the height of a summer storm, none of them lingering for more than a brief second for closer examination, but all of them doing tremendous damage to the areas they had struck.

With his conclusions drawn, Alastair had no hint of what to do next. He could hardly stand up straight, announce his true identity, and then accuse her of attempted murder. But, while they played the roles of devoted sister and injured veteran, he could not act on his greatest impulse—which was to pull her along with him to some secluded spot beneath the cliff and spend a pleasurable hour investigating her for other hidden areas of beauty.

Not only that, but he had to remain friendly toward her, so that he could get back into Seashadow and examine the half dozen volumes of Lowell family history for mention of the Dalrymples. He had honestly believed himself to be the last of his line, with his title to pass either to the crown or into eternity along with him if he died without issue, and could not rid himself of the nagging feeling that Elinor Dalrymple had stepped in before his body could even be found and somehow hoodwinked his solicitors into believing a false claim to the title.

Good God! She might even, if he were to stretch the point, be one of the spies Wiggins was hunting, and his own murder was the means her gang of cutthroats had employed to gain free access to Seashadow. The possibilities were limitless! He'd have to suggest this last thought to Wiggins once the man returned from London.

So how was he to remain on good terms with the woman—would she for the love of heaven stop looking at him that way!—and not insult her by refusing what it was so obvious she was offering?

Taking a deep breath, Alastair uttered the fatal words he had not thought to hear himself say to anyone for at least five more glorious, responsibility-free years: "Miss Dalrymple, would it seem too forward, too optimistic on my part, if I were to believe I might be allowed to speak to your brother? I am not a rich man, but I come from a good, honest family...." He allowed his voice to die away, as he was actually beginning to feel physically ill.

He watched as a shiver—of surprise? of shock? of anticipation?—shook her slim body. "You wish to—to *court* me, John? This is so—so *unexpected*. I should never had let down my hair, but you were all but *dar-*

ing me to prove that—I *am* in mourning, you understand—"

Dropping the cane on the sand, he grabbed her hands and held them tight against his chest, feeling like an actor caught up in a bad play. "In mourning, yes—for a distant relation you loathed," Alastair reminded her, trying not to grit his teeth. "I am attracted to you—deeply attracted to you. Come, dear Elly," he prodded, daringly, "don't say that you aren't attracted to me. You let your hair down for me. Admit to our mutual attraction, and we can go on from there."

He let go of her hands, bent to retrieve the cane, and turned to limp away, his head bowed, his entire posture one of hurt, of defeat. "I have overstepped," he intoned sorrowfully. "I am a Nothing, a Nobody—begging favors from the sister of an Earl. You are right to refuse me, Miss Dalrymple. Please disregard the happenings of these past minutes. I shall try to do likewise, although it will be the most difficult thing I have ever done—that I will ever do."

He felt her hand touch his shoulder and nearly laughed aloud in relief. She had actually believed him! He should try his talents on the boards; it was possible he was another, but more handsome, Edmund Kean!

"Please, John," he heard her say as she tugged at his shoulder, "don't feel hurt. I didn't mean to upset you. It's just…well, it's just that this is so sudden. One moment we were bickering and the next you were on the verge of declaring yourself. My head is spinning."

She didn't mean to upset me? What did she think she was going to do to him by turning from spinster to Come-Hither-Incomparable in front of his eyes—

leave him unmoved? He was supposedly recovering from a war wound—not fighting off senility!

And did he detect a small note of placation in her voice, a hint of deliberate cajoling? Was she really attracted to him or did she have another motive? It wasn't in her nature to be so nice to him—not if his previous encounters with her were to be used as a yardstick with which to measure her reaction now. Perhaps she thought to recruit him to her gang of spies?

Alastair's head was beginning to pound with all of his jumbled thinking. It was time to end this conversation, this tense moment that had already gone on too long. Turning about, he took her hand and began walking back down the beach, idly noting that Leslie and Hugo had disappeared somewhere or other and were no longer visible.

"I think we two should separate and privately reflect on what has passed between us this afternoon, Miss Dalrymple. Then, later, over dinner at Seashadow, perhaps—and with your brother the Earl present as vigilant chaperone—we can reevaluate our reactions." There—that hadn't sounded as if he had deliberately tried to wrangle another invitation to dinner.

She nodded vigorously, removing her hand from his so that she could begin to repin her hair—making Alastair feel as if the sun, which was still burning brightly high in the sky, had suddenly disappeared behind a cloud. "I could not agree more, John," she told him briskly, her mouth full of hairpins as she struggled to fix the mass of tangled gold into a clumsy yet attractive topknot. "And, please, you called me Elly in the heat of the—that is, would you please continue to address me informally? Miss Dalrymple seems so needlessly stilted now.''

Alastair put his hand lightly, unthreateningly, against her slim back as they walked in the direction of Seashadow, his cane punching small circles in the sand with every step. ''You are too kind, Elly,'' he said, silently thanking whatever lucky star he was born under for her willingness to go along with his plan, no matter what her motives. ''Are you aware, Elly, that Saltwood Castle is nearby?''

She didn't disappoint him, but readily accepted his giant leap of conversation from the extraordinary to the mundane. ''No, I did not know. Wasn't that once used by the Archbishop of Canterbury?''

''And as the rendezvous of the murderers of poor Becket before they did the dastardly deed,'' Alastair confirmed, smiling down at her. She really was an intelligent puss—intelligent enough to be everything he supposed her to be and more. ''Hythe, I have found since coming to Kent to nurse my wounds, is a treasure trove of history—and me with only a few books in the cottage. Perhaps you will allow me to run tame in Seashadow's library, so that I might try to increase my knowledge?'' he put out hopefully.

''I should be honored. Seashadow has an extensive collection of histories,'' Elly replied, smiling up at him, allowing Alastair to smile openly at what he believed to be his brilliant ploy for getting himself a step closer to the Lowell family histories.

''Let me think of other things I have learned about this area. There is a church built much along the lines of Canterbury Cathedral that contains a crypt boasting a huge collection of bones and skulls of what the book called 'sketchy' origin,'' he went on encouragingly. ''And of course, there is also Studfall Castle, site of an ancient Roman camp...''

HE WAS SUCH a lovely man, this Leslie was; kind, and gentle. A lot like his ma, come to think on it. Only, his ma didn't smile so much—or talk so much without really saying anything.

Hugo's massive brow puckered as he pondered the differences between the Earl of Hythe and his deceased mother, but he couldn't think about it for very long, because Leslie was talking at him again and he knew he should listen.

''This promontory, Hugo, is where I should like to pose you with the butterfly,'' Leslie informed his companion, puffing slightly as Hugo, with his hands on his lordship's derriere, helped push the man up the remainder of the hill to the cliff.

''Thank you, Hugo. I hadn't realized it was such a climb. But here we are now, aren't we? With the trees to one side, and all God's infinity to the other, it is the perfect place for what I have in mind. Don't you think so, my friend?''

Hugo, having gained the top of the hill himself, looked about inquiringly, wondering just what a promontory might be and if he should recognize it when he spied it, then gurgled and nodded his agreement The Earl might be a mite strange, but Hugo, who had experienced too little friendship in his life, would have followed the man into the fires of Hell with a smile on his face.

''Of course,'' Leslie went on, excitement building in his voice, ''I shall have you—or should I say, your hands, for that is all of you that is necessary to this particular creation—several times the size of the trees. I think I shall use three trees. Yes, three trees exactly. I like working in threes, you understand.''

As Leslie talked, he walked, his thin arms flailing in the breeze as inspiration followed hard on inspiration. Hugo watched, entranced by the frail man in full creative spate, then looked down at his hard, callused hands, once more wondering what it could be that Leslie saw in them that had excited him so. After all, they were only hands, and dirty hands at that, with broken and chewed nails. He couldn't talk with them, could he? He'd give one of them up most happily if he could but be given a tongue in exchange.

Leslie was standing close to the end of the cliff, *his* tongue still going sixteen to the dozen about ''space'' and ''infinity'' and ''the great power of the sea.'' Hugo didn't understand more than every third word, but he certainly did enjoy hearing the sound of Leslie's cultured voice as it rose above the crash of surf against the rocks at the base of the cliff.

''Your hands, Hugo, will be floating somewhere toward the middle of the picture, the butterfly cupped in your joined palms, just so,'' Leslie continued, cupping his own hands as he demonstrated what he had in mind. ''I should like the sun coming over your left shoulder—not that your shoulder will be there, of course, but I'm speaking figuratively. Oh, dear, you're frowning. Am I confusing you again, my friend? Not to worry. You'll understand when you see it.''

Hugo doubted that, but he flashed his gap-toothed grin and nodded vigorously, his smile fading only as Leslie turned and took another step toward the edge of the cliff, his eyes on the horizon. *"Aaaarrgh,"* Hugo warned quietly, advancing toward the Earl before the man slipped and tumbled to his death.

"What's that, Hugo?" Leslie asked.

As Leslie hesitated, Hugo's keen eyes caught the glint of something shiny among the trees to his right. A half heartbeat later, as Leslie was turning to look at Hugo, a very large, very dangerous-looking knife came winging out of the trees, to sail harmlessly past the Earl's shoulder and arc gracefully into the sea.

Hugo squeezed his eyes shut and shook his head. Had he really seen what he thought he had seen? He opened his eyes once more to see that Leslie was standing in front of him, saying something about painting the sea full of frogs, to represent the threat from the French, while filling the trees with snakes, and carrion crows, to signify—well, they would signify something. He'd figure out precisely what as he went along. Not all art was the result of instant inspiration. "What do you think, Hugo?" The Earl ended, hands on hips.

Hugo didn't think. Hugo *couldn't* think—he was too terrified at the realization that he had almost been witness to the death of his new friend. But, most important of all, he couldn't *speak*. He couldn't communicate what he had seen other than by acting it out—and Leslie Dalrymple could be murdered three times over until he could make him understand that he was in danger.

Yes, Hugo knew he could only do one thing—and so he did it. He lifted the astonished Earl over his shoulder as if he were no heavier than a sackful of feathers and ran as fast as he could down the hill toward Alastair, his deep, booming voice—filled with unintelligible urgency—preceding him down the length of the beach.

ELLY ALLOWED John's hand to remain lightly at her waist as they walked back up the beach in companionable silence, content to concentrate on the satisfaction she would feel once he was exposed for what he was and clapped in irons. So lost was she in this pleasant daydream that it took several seconds for the unearthly wail to invade her mind, and by then John had already begun racing full tilt up the beach ahead of her, leaving his cane behind.

"Oh, good lord, John, what is that terrible caterwauling?" she called after him, hitching up her skirts and breaking into a run herself.

"It's Hugo!" John called over his shoulders as his long legs ate up the grounds. He all but flew over it, his coattails flapping behind him in the breeze. "Something's wrong!" He disappeared around an outcropping of rocks that marked a turn in the beach.

"Leslie!" Elly fairly screamed, her heart pounding hurtfully somewhere in her throat as she skidded to a halt on the soft sand, her feet suddenly incapable of further movement. Yes, she had noticed that John had given up his pretense of a limp, but for the moment that didn't matter a jot. Hugo was in trouble, and Leslie was with Hugo! There must have been an accident!

"Oh, please, God, let him be all right," she begged, wiping sudden tears from her cheeks with trembling fingers. "If you let him be all right, I promise not to let him out of my sight ever, ever again. If you let him be all right, I'll turn the information I've discovered over to Lieutenant Fishbourne and—and put on my caps and learn to knit properly! I'll do good works in all the local villages, Lord. I'll—oh, thank God, *Leslie!*"

"Elly!" the Earl piped up gaily, trotting toward her from around the rocks. "It was the oddest thing. One moment I was discussing my ideas with Hugo and the next he was lifting me on his shoulder and running with me down the beach—screeching like a banshee. Do you think it was some primitive expression of joy because I want to paint him? Ah well, it was exhilarating, to say the least."

Leslie stopped in front of her to straighten his disheveled clothing before looking at his sister. "Good gracious, Elly, get a grip on yourself. You look as if you've seen a ghost. And I thought the sea air would put some color in your cheeks."

She didn't know if she wanted to kiss him or box his ears. Not only had he scared her half to death, he was insulting her for looking as if she had just been frightened out of ten years of her life—which she had. Deciding it was better to distance herself from her brother for a few moments while she searched for composure, she walked past him to where John and Hugo were standing, deep in conversation.

At least John was conversing. Hugo was gesturing furiously, demonstrating by use of his entire massive body what had transpired that had brought him to lose himself to the point where he would manhandle an Earl.

"Yes, yes, I think I see what you mean," she heard John say as she approached. "You're a cliff, right?

Good. Well, since you couldn't actually *be* a cliff, you must mean you were *on* a cliff.''

Hugo grunted, his massive arms flailing wildly as he began to prance back and forth across the sand. He appeared almost light-footed for all his hugeness as he continued to race up and down the beach, looking like a flightless bird or—to Elly's mind—a pachyderm attempting ballet.

''Correction,'' John continued with a noticeable hint of humor in his voice, watching the giant's ungainly dance. ''You *and the Earl* were on the cliff.''

''Wretch,'' Elly said quietly, silently agreeing with John's deduction. If one could mentally deduct about two-thirds of Hugo's weight, he was Leslie to the life!

The giant nodded to John, then began performing in a way that looked to Elly as if he were attempting to demonstrate something between drawing a line in the air and his own rendition of the death scene in *Romeo and Juliet*.

''I have to own it, Hugo,'' she heard John say, ''you have totally lost me on this one. I haven't the faintest idea what you're talking about. And why were you carrying the Earl when I found you?''

Elly felt a cold horror invade her chest. ''Leslie was running about...full of himself and his new idea... and...and he nearly toppled over the cliff! Oh, of course, what else could it be?'' She advanced on Hugo, intending to thank him for saving her brother, but the large man eluded her, shaking his head, becoming increasingly breathless as he continued to act out his explanation.

''Yes, yes, Hugo,'' she soothed, taking hold of his hand, ''I understand completely. There's no need to exert yourself further. My brother must have frightened you extremely—so much so that you grabbed him up and ran back to us just as quickly as you could. Oh, Hugo, you are a hero!''

"Aaaarrrggh!" Hugo groaned, lifting his massive hands, palms up, before turning to John, as if begging for help.

"Don't be modest, my friend. I already have reason to know what a hero you are. I couldn't agree with Miss Dalrymple more, Hugo, and I think you behaved admirably,'' John answered before turning to Elly. "Have you ever considered keeping Leslie on leading strings, Elly? It might save everyone a lot of bother.''

For once Elly didn't mind that someone had insulted her brother, because she agreed with John completely. This wasn't the first time since arriving at Seashadow that Leslie had escaped a near disaster. There had been the toadstools he'd purchased from some traveling merchant while out for a walk and nearly ingested before Big George could stop him—and the morning he had been walking on the beach near the cliff and a loose rock had fallen not two feet form his head.

"Now what is he about, do you suppose?''

Elly looked at John, to see that he was looking past her to Leslie—who was walking toward the path that led up to Seashadow, his arms waving wildly, deep in conversation with himself. He was off on another of his tangents, she was sure of it, leaving her to find her own way home. "There are times I could absolutely *choke* that boy!'' she said feelingly.

"Really?''

"Don't be ridiculous.'' She didn't understand the tone of John's voice. It was almost as if he actually believed her capable of murder. Looking over her shoulder at him as she started after her brother, she said, ''We'll expect you later this evening for dinner, John. And, oh, yes, I'm so glad to see that your leg is better.'' She watched as he looked down at his legs, then across the beach to where his cane lay, forgotten.

''Well, stap me if it isn't! I guess it was a miracle,'' Elly heard him say weakly as she walked away, already planning her next move meant to expose his real identity—all earlier pleas and promises to her Maker forgotten.

CHAPTER FOUR

ELLY WAS WELL pleased with the furnishings at Seashadow, handsome yet functional furniture that reflected the exemplary taste of the previous Earl—
which was the *only* good thing she had been able to
attribute to that man since she had first learned of his
existence.

The Rudd's Reflecting Dressing Table in her own
Dresden blue and white boudoir was, however, her
particular favorite. The Hepplewhite piece had been
meticulously designed with an abundance of intri-
cately compartmented drawers to hold her meager sup-
ply of beauty aids. But for sheer genius of design,
nothing could surpass the arrangement of not one, but
two mirrors that could be adjusted to endless posi-
tions—obviously fashioned to provide milady with
limitless views of her person.

And for the past fifteen minutes Elly had been doing
just that—examining her reflection from every possible angle—while at the same time trying desperately
to convince herself it mattered not a jot to her if her
scalloped lace hem was dragging, or her ruched
sleeves uneven, or her hair (which she had combed
over the curling stick until it was turned into a mass
of curls) was too high, or her cheeks were too pale.

The gown she had chosen for the evening, an incredibly soft butter-yellow silk, had not been worn since Robert's death three years previously and was most woefully out-of-date, even for her, but it was the best she could do. The best she wished to do. It had been Robert's favorite, and besides, it wasn't as if it would send her into a rapid decline if a certain Mister John Bates didn't swoon with ecstasy at the sight of the thing.

Yet, it was her complexion that bothered her most, if the truth were to be told. Leaning forward, and adjusting the small brace of candles that stood on the dressing table, she turned her face this way and that, wondering if she dared to touch her too pale cheeks with a discreet dusting of rouge. She wanted to keep John's interest, but she didn't want it to be too obvious that she was all but throwing herself at his head.

She leaned closer to the mirrors and compromised by pinching her cheeks tightly between thumbs and forefingers, the stinging pain immediately bringing tears to her eyes. The pain also brought her crashing back to reality. What in the name of all that she held dear was she doing?

"John Bates means nothing to me—*less* than nothing! I don't believe his protestations of affection for a moment. As if he had *really* been suddenly struck with love the moment I let my hair down on the beach. It sounds like something out of a silly novel. Well, he doesn't fool me. He only wishes to ingratiate himself at Seashadow so that he can carry on his nefarious exploits without fear that I—his besotted slave—will be capable of seeing past the tip of my own infatuated nose to discover what he is really about."

This said—and said with admirable conviction—

Elly gave the twin mirrors a determined push, so that all they reflected was a view of the stuccoed ceiling, and turned her back on Mister Rudd's versatile dressing table.

She stiffened her spine and her resolve, determined not to succumb to charm, or fancy words, or even longing looks from hypnotic grey eyes—all of which she was convinced she was about to receive from the hardened seducer she had already kept waiting downstairs for well above fifteen minutes.

There was a knock at the door to the hallway, and Lily Biggs entered the boudoir before Elly could give permission for her to do so. Holding on to the doorknob with one hand while the other rested indolently on her thrust-out hip, the girl looked her mistress up and down in an openly assessing manner that had Elly wishing she had chosen the drab chimney-smoke muslin rather than the more daring yellow silk.

"Don't yer look as spiffy as the kitchen cat's whiskers?" Lily commented at last, her expression one Elly would have put down to pure female jealousy if the girl had been older than sixteen. "I bin sent ter fetch yer, missy. His lordship said fer me to tell yer he's waiting, and Da says the pigeons are gonna go straight to Hell fer sure iffen yer don't put yer feet under the table soon."

"Inform my brother that I shall be down directly, please, Lily," Elly said as calmly as she could while hastily readjusting the mirrors so that she could give one last assessing look at the rather low neckline of her gown.

"Him? And wot does *he* care when you—oh, yeah,

right," the girl replied, backing from the room. "Yer brother. I'll tell him, too."

"And don't swear, Lily," Elly added absently, biting her lip as she leaned forward to see that, yes, there was just a hint of cleavage visible above the silk. It was too much. She wanted to entice John, and for reasons of his own he seemed willing to allow her to believe he had been enticed, but she didn't want him to think she was about to throw propriety to the winds just because he wished to court her.

After all, when this was over and he was being hauled off to the local guardhouse, she also didn't want him to be able to find solace in the sure knowledge that, although he had failed in his spying mission, he had succeeded in making a complete fool out of a gullible spinster—who would most probably wear the willow for him to her grave.

So thinking, she ruthlessly rifled through her armoire until she found the ivory cashmere shawl that had been her last present from Robert. Draping it modestly about her shoulders, she took a deep, steadying breath and headed for the long staircase, knowing she was as ready as she would ever be to do battle with the handsome, infuriating John Bates.

ALASTAIR FOUGHT the urge to make a detour between the dining room and drawing room to visit the kitchens and plant a smacking kiss on Big George's cheek in appreciation of an excellent dinner. It had been, in fact, the first truly edible—or at least completely *identifiable*—meal he'd had since waking in Hugo's hovel.

Of course, the pigeons had been a mite overdone, he remembered as he straddled his favorite Sheraton conversation chair—an inspired, round-seated convenience with its abbreviated back serving as its front so that a gentleman could sit comfortably without crushing his coattails—and faced his host and hostess. But the trout Madère had more than made up for this single lapse.

His host and hostess, he saw, had already made themselves comfortable on the settee. What a diverse pair they were, these two Dalrymples, no matter that they were both blonde—which was, Alastair remembered uncomfortably, a Lowell family trait.

Not, he went on mentally as he watched Elly pour tea, that blondes were so scarce on the ground in England that being blonde could be used as proof of their right to inherit Seashadow. Besides, he knew it as a fact that a woman's hair color was not always what it appeared to be. Her brows and lashes were dark, after all. The next time dear Miss Dalrymple took down her hair to play the coquette, he'd be well advised to take a long peek at her roots.

"You don't care for tea, John?" Elly said as he waved his hand to turn down her offer to pour a cup for him.

"Truth to tell, Elly," he said as brightly as possible, "I'd much rather have a brandy—for medicinal purposes, of course. My leg is paying me back for that run I took on the beach today, although I've consigned my cane to the corner at last." His eyes slid to the far corner of the drawing room and the sideboard hiding a cellarette that, at least during his tenure at Seashadow, had contained no less than an even dozen wine bottles at all times.

Leslie hopped to his feet. "Of course you do,

John," he agreed happily. "I should have thought of it m'self, except that I don't really drink. Well, not that I don't know *how* to drink, or get all silly or weepy when I do, but I never really liked the taste of the stuff. Elly," he questioned, turning to his sister, "where do we keep the brandy?"

Elly looked at Alastair, her slanted brown eyes narrowed speculatively. "John, do you want to show him, or shall I?"

"Me?" Alastair exclaimed, silently cursing himself for a dolt and his hostess for an all-seeing witch. "Oh, very well," he agreed, rising as his agile brain quickly scrambled for and found a reasonable explanation for his potentially disastrous faux pas. "I must admit I had done a spot of reconnoitering while waiting for you to join us for dinner. I think there may be some brandy in this lovely piece over here in the corner."

"That's true enough, Elly," Leslie supplied, unknowingly earning himself Alastair's grateful thanks. "You took dashed long answering the dinner bell, not that it wasn't worth the wait. You don't look half so bad in yellow as you do in black."

Alastair turned to the sideboard to hide his smile. Poor Miss Dalrymple. No wonder she had turned to a life of crime, if she would have otherwise had to depend on her brother for financial support. The youth was amusing, to say the least, but his talent for plain speech wasn't exactly marketable.

"Ah," he said, opening the japanned doors and sliding out the built-in cellarette that moved on well-oiled rollers, "here we are. Lord Hythe, would you care to join me in a snifter? Brandy is an acquired taste, after all, and you may just have given up before your palate learned to enjoy it.''

"My brother does not drink," Elly declared coldly, and Alastair was instantly glad that it was he and not she who was standing at the sideboard which was, he knew, fully supplied with many things, including a fine set of very sharp knives.

She certainly was protective of her brother—either that or she was angry that they had spent the entire dinner talking of the weather, without a single mention of Alastair's intention to ask permission to court her.

No, that couldn't be it. She didn't really want him— he was convinced of that. She wanted something from him, but he couldn't bring himself to believe it was romance. Why, the way she looked at him when she thought he wasn't looking back made him believe she'd rather have his head on a pike than his ring on her finger.

"Brandy costs too much, for one thing," Leslie groused, shifting in his seat and unknowingly bringing Alastair's mind back to the present. "But, Elly, now that I'm rich, don't you think—"

"No, I don't think," Elly cut in quickly. Her voice lowered to a near whisper. "Remember Papa, Leslie?"

"Drank like a fish," Leslie observed, nodding his head and looking, to Alastair's eyes, more envious than crestfallen as Alastair settled himself once more on the conversation chair to warm the brandy by rubbing the snifter between his palms. "He was a lot of fun when he was in his cups," the young man went on, confirming Alastair's assumption. "Bought me a pony once—though we had to sell it a fortnight later to pay the butcher or some such thing. Excalibur. That's what I called him—the pony, not Papa. Papa thought it was a good name, didn't he Elly?''

''I don't think John is interested in hearing about our late father, Leslie,'' Elly said, a little tight-lipped, although her cheeks were glowing a becoming pink.

So, Alastair thought, looking at his quarry as he allowed the first of the brandy to sear the back of his throat, it would appear I have stumbled onto another sore point. Perhaps the late Mister Dalrymple bears further exploration.

Aloud, he said sympathetically, ''You have lost your father and mother as well, haven't you, Elly— and now the late Earl. It's a terrible thing, isn't it, how tragedies seem to come in threes?''

''I like threes,'' Leslie piped up happily, before interesting himself in a loose thread on his shirt cuff.

''Three deaths over the course of twenty years could hardly be considered an unending run of tragedy, John,'' Elly said, her fingers pleating and repleating a section of her skirt as she looked at her brother. ''Our mother died in childbirth many years ago, and our father expired five years ago. As for the late Earl—''

''Yes, yes, I know,'' Alastair cut in, knowing he was not going to be able to hear her disparage his memory another time without longing to take her over his knee and deliver a few hard whacks to her uncaring posterior, ''you did not know him and have not liked anything you've learned about him.''

''Well, I like him,'' Leslie put in staunchly, earning Alastair's at least momentary adoration. ''He left us all his lovely money, and Seashadow, and at least two other, even larger estates—Elly knows more about that sort of thing than I do, of course—and all his furniture, and his townhouse in London...and the Biggses.'' Leslie's smile broadened as he rubbed his stomach reflectively. "I think I like the Biggses best of all, come to think on it.''

"Big George does have quite a wonderful way in the kitchens,'' Alastair agreed, liking Leslie more than he knew he should. Perhaps it was because he knew the youth to be too hopelessly naive to be involved in any terrible conspiracy—or perhaps it was simply because Leslie Dalrymple, unlike his prickly sister, was just a very likable person.

Or maybe, Alastair considered briefly, it is because I have gone stark, staring mad! "I know Hugo was over the moon when I told him we'd be returning here for dinner tonight,'' he added, feeling he had to say something.

Leslie nodded emphatically. "Good food is essential to happiness, John—and to creativity. Why, I think I have had more inspiration from Big George's strawberry pancakes than I ever had from Nellie's cooking.''

"Nellie?'' Alastair interposed, raising one eyebrow as he looked at Elly. "You didn't bring your own servant with you to Seashadow? Perhaps she was older, and didn't wish to leave her home. Where was it that you said you were from, originally?''

"North,'' Elly answered without telling him anything. A toothdrawer wouldn't be able to get anything out of her!

"Nellie's been gone six months or more,'' Leslie explained as his sister's elbow dug deeply into his waist. "Ow, Elly, stop that, do. John was just asking a question. We couldn't afford her anymore, Elly said. Not that I miss her. I tell you, John, it was insupportable!"

"She stole from you?" Alastair asked idly, beginning to lose interest in the conversation that, he could tell, was not going in any helpful direction. He'd had more invigorating conversations at funerals.

"Exactly! She ate the fruit arrangement I was painting—with Napoleon's face hidden in the wicker basket and all the fruit shaped just like the countries he has conquered. Took a whacking huge bite from Egypt, she did. Egypt—it was the pear. There was no way to hide it, so I had to abandon the project."

"Have another cup of tea, darling," Elly gritted through clenched teeth, obviously trying another avenue meant to shut up her brother before he could drag out any more of their personal family laundry for Alastair's inspection.

Alastair took another deep sip of brandy, knowing this talk of sacked servants and strawberry pancakes and Napoleonic pears was the oddest after-dinner conversation he had ever had, and waited to see what would happen next.

To Alastair's amusement, Elly's two obvious bids to silence her brother were both immediate and dismal failures. Leslie, who seemed to have the bit firmly between his teeth, was not to be distracted by either physical attack or offers of refreshment.

"Nellie was the only real servant we ever had, you understand," Leslie reported, as if explaining himself to a schoolmaster. "Elly has taken care of us all for as long as I can remember. Cheap as a clipped farthing, our Elly is, or so Papa always said."

As he watched embarrassed color flood Elly's face, Alastair was hit with a sudden, entirely uncharacteristic urge to rescue her from her brother's indiscreet mouth—although why he should feel this compassion for the woman, he had no idea.

"Leslie," he broke in just as that man was about to open his mouth once more and say something most probably directed toward explaining his sister's cheese-paring ways, "I couldn't help but admire the large oil painting in the dining room as we sat at table. It's a truly glorious landscape of this area of Kent, don't you think?"

Leslie's thin nose wrinkled, just as if he had suddenly smelled something rotten. "You liked that, John? Yes, well," he went on blithely, "there's no accounting for tastes, is there?"

"What's wrong with it?" Alastair was stung into asking for he had commissioned the painting himself, and it was a particular favorite of his.

"It's too ordinary," Leslie answered, taking another sip of tea.

"But it's a landscape," Alastair persisted, the insult to his taste—which had been touted in London as being nothing short of exquisite—overriding his need for caution. "What did you want, man—pink leaves and red grass?"

"Pink leaves?" Leslie questioned softly, his thin, artistic face lighting with inspiration. "Pink leaves." He rose from the settee, his sister taking the teacup from him before it could slip from his hand, and left the room, muttering over and over, "Pink leaves. Yes, I can see them. Pink leaves."

Alastair and Elly watched him go, the former shaking his head in wonderment, the latter wearing a look that could only be called long-suffering.

"I suppose you think he's insane and I should have had him put away years ago," Elly said at last, turning back to Alastair.

"I didn't mean to set him off, Elly," Alastair began apologetically, for the hurt in her eyes was doing something very disturbing to his resolve to unmask her as a criminal. As a matter of fact, the way he felt now, for two pins he'd throw the whole thing up, confess his true identity, and have done with this increasingly intricate madness.

"At least he stayed for tea. He doesn't usually last this long," she told him, not making him feel any better.

"And I didn't even get to speak to him about my intentions," he added, that thought suddenly striking him, for although he would have liked to forget the scene on the beach, he was likewise aware that he could not do so and retain any credibility in Elinor Dalrymple's too keen eyes.

"You mean you still wish to pay court to me?" Elly asked, one slim hand going to her hair. He knew he should have commented on its looser, more attractive style, just as he should have complimented her on her ridiculously out-of-date yet becoming gown, but he also was aware that he had left it too late.

"Why shouldn't I, Elly?" he asked, scrambling to recall what it was like to try to insinuate himself with an innocent female. The redhead, and her small legion of predecessors—who had made up the majority of his female acquaintance for the past several years—had left him woefully out of practice for dealing with the tedious game of lighthearted flirtation. For Alastair, the gift of a strand of pearls or a diamond brooch had taken the place of flirtation, and he hadn't been disappointed with the results—until now.

He had burst upon the scene in London the year after his father's death, a raw enough youth with no real social graces, although his fortune and pretty face had gone a long way in gaining him entry to any level of society he chose.

His interests, physical inclination, and athletic prowess had naturally drawn him to the Corinthian set, so that he had adopted that group's disdain for tame entertainments. Indeed, Alastair's quest to enliven boring *ton* functions, when combined with his audacious conversation, had more than once sent the more gentle ladies searching in their reticules for restoratives.

Strangely, as he sat in his own drawing room in Seashadow, he felt more embarrassed than comforted by his remembrance of his life in London.

Once he was back in the city, he'd have to curtail his visits to his clubs and pay more attention to Almack's and all those insipid balls he's shunned so disdainfully in favor of more robust entertainment. After all, he was seven and twenty now, and he really should try to cultivate some decorum.

Elinor Dalrymple's poor opinion of him had not been sharp enough to wound him (or so he tried to convince himself), but the sure knowledge that she was only voicing the sentiments of many of the more acceptable members of Polite Society did rankle more than he cared to admit.

He should have gone to Spain, he told himself, sipping at his brandy. Many of his friends had gone. And it wasn't as if he were a coward, afraid of spilling his claret for his King and country. He had wanted to go, to follow the drum. But the war was winding down—everyone had said so—and it had seemed that Wellington and the others had everything pretty much in hand.

Oh, yes, he had taken up his seat in Parliament, and had fought mightily for better provisions and pay for the soldiers in the field—and why hadn't Elly heard of that and tempered her disdain with some compassion?—but it wasn't quite the same as actually *being* there, and Alastair knew it.

That was probably why he had leapt at the chance to help Wiggins when that man had approached him. Why else had he been on his yacht, with his course already set for Seashadow from Folkestone, when he was dumped overboard to drown? He might have allowed Wiggins to think he'd had no intention of taking an active part in apprehending the spy, but deep in his heart of hearts he knew he had wanted to be in on the kill.

"John? Are you all right?" he heard Elly ask in a voice that sounded muffled, as if he were hearing it from a distance. He shook his head, bringing his attention back to her as she continued, "I know Leslie is a bit peculiar, and I quite understand if you wish to rethink your decision to ask him if you might pay your addresses to me—"

"What does your brother have to do with the thing?" Alastair asked, for she was confusing him. Why was she carrying on about Leslie? Why was it that a woman always felt she had the obligation to talk a thing to death? He had already told her he thought Leslie was a good enough sort.

He watched as Elly lowered her head, so that the candlelight was caught in the soft curls that crowned her head. "At home, Leslie was spoken of as...as the resident freak."

Alastair was instantly irate. No wonder she was worrying the subject—she was harboring a great hurt. Poor girl! Poor Leslie!

"People can be so damnably cruel, Elly," he said savagely, stung by the vehemence in his voice. "Your brother is anything but a freak. As I told you before— he is an eccentric. As far as I can tell, this whole island is awash in them. Why, I myself had an uncle who thought he was Alexander the Great. He was always racing about, hot to conquer things. Yet, for all of that, he was a good man and I loved him dearly."

"But—but there might be a *taint,* some sort of strain of eccentricity, as you call it, that runs through the entire family. My mother was a Lowell—which is how we came to be here—and she married my father, which just goes to prove that she had an odd way of looking at life."

"Your mother was like Leslie?" Alastair asked, beginning to feel real sympathy for Elly, and silently thanking his lucky stars that, if they were indeed related—which he was nearly convinced they were not—it was a distant relationship.

She bit her lip. "In her own way. Mama wrote poetry—her favorite subject was the supernatural. She was convinced that there exists a parallel world full of ghosts and spirits and the like. Supposedly they move all around us, eating and sleeping and doing everything we do. It's just that we can't see them.''

Well, Alastair thought, that knocks my uncle out of the running for the strangest person this side of Bedlam. "And your father?" he asked weakly, not really sure he wished to know.

"My father, rest his soul, was a gambler. Oh, how I hate to say that word aloud. The man would invest in anything—including those horrid bubbles that everyone thought were going to make them rich. Leslie may call me cheap, but it was very difficult to run the household and still keep Papa out of the Fleet. Oh, why am I telling you all this?''

Alastair couldn't answer her, because he was as completely at sea as she admitted to being as to why she was revealing her past to him. He only knew that every word out of her mouth could only serve to further damn her in his eyes—if his belief that she was a money-grubbing opportunist was to be his guide.

All he could do was rise from his chair, place his now empty snifter on the table beside the teacups, seat himself on the settee, his arm placed tentatively but supportively across her shoulders, and listen to what she had to say.

"We were living most precariously on less than two hundred pounds a year," she went on, searching in her gown pocket for a small linen handkerchief with which to wipe at her eyes. Alastair deliberately looked straight ahead, knowing that her exotic brown eyes were awash with tears, and the sight of them might prompt him into doing something stupid, like kissing her.

"Even with Papa gone, his debts didn't disappear.

A debt of honor must be paid, you know, and I couldn't allow Papa's memory to be besmirched by any rumor that he hadn't settled his gambling debts.''

''Debts of honor can be the very devil,'' Alastair agreed sincerely, having paid a few of them himself over the years.

''You can't imagine the pucker we were in before the solicitor told us of Leslie's inheritance. Turning Nellie off was the last of our little economies. I had no idea where I was going to get the next quarter's rent.''

''Why—why didn't you apply to the late Earl for assistance?'' he asked dumbly, remembering too late that she hadn't known of his existence.

He felt her spine stiffen as pride, it would appear, suddenly came to her rescue. ''I would never have thought of such a thing—even if I had known about him!'' she asserted haughtily. ''I have looked over his books, John, since coming to Seashadow. Why, his expenditures on candles alone would be enough to keep Leslie and me in comfort for a decade! What could a hey-go-mad spendthrift like that understand of our problems?''

Alastair's arm slipped to the back of the settee. What was ten times two hundred? Good Lord! He'd spent that much on candles? It was impossible! To spend that much on horses, or fine wine, or brandy—that was one thing. But to spend it on *candles?* He was pretty angry with the late Earl of Hythe himself! With spendthrift habits like that, why, it wouldn't be long before he was out on the street, begging passersby for stale crusts of bread!

''You've suffered, Elly, haven't you?'' he commiserated feelingly, his arm once more draped across her shoulder. The cashmere shawl had shifted, and he liked the soft, silken feel of her bare shoulder. A man could do a lot worse than to get himself a wife who was such a sensible, economical housekeeper. After all, somebody had to keep a rein on expenses, and according to Leslie, Elly could squeeze a pennypiece until it yelped in pain.

She sat front, dislodging his arm. "It wasn't that bad, John," she said, blowing her nose before replacing the handkerchief in her pocket. "Besides, that is all behind us now, thanks to Alastair Lowell's drunkenness."

Alastair's ears pricked up—he could swear he felt them move. "His *drunkenness?*"

Elly nodded. "I had a missive from his solicitor this morning. The final ruling on his death was just what we all supposed—that he had been drunk and must have stumbled overboard. It seems that he was playing at cards until nearly dawn, and drinking with both hands. He died, John, as he had lived—and with nothing to show for his life."

She turned to face him and he did his best to close his mouth, which had dropped open as she spoke. "That is why I am so glad that I am here to guide Leslie. He has a heavy responsibility as Earl—the first of which is to marry to ensure the line."

Drunk? The world thought he had been drunk? He hadn't been drunk—well, maybe a little well to go, but not drunk! Surely he hadn't been *drunk!*

"Which is why," she went on, her voice suddenly very low, "I must decline your suggestion that we entertain the thought that the two of us might suit. I cannot marry, even if you are willing to overlook a possible Lowell taint. I cannot leave Leslie now. But that doesn't mean that we can't be friends while you are here, does it. John? John, have you heard a single word I've said?''

She was turning him down! She thought he was a rakehell, the whole world and his wife thought he had drunkenly fallen overboard, he had never made a worthwhile contribution to mankind in all his twenty-seven years, he spent money on candles like a drunken lighthouse keeper on a spree—and a plainfaced, firmly on-the-shelf spinster who was kissing her last chance for marriage goodbye *was turning him down flat!*

Alastair needed a drink. He got up from the settee, caught up his snifter, and fairly stumbled to the sideboard to pour himself three fingers of brandy—which he tossed off in one long gulp.

''You're hurt, aren't you?'' he heard Elly say, as if from a distance.

''Hurt?'' he repeated, whirling about to stab her with his steely grey gaze—the brandy he had imbibed nearly causing him to lose his balance. He had to say one thing for the woman—she certainly did have an eye for the obvious. ''Madam, you are mistaken,'' he declared, his voice dripping with venom.

''I am?''

''Yes, you am—I mean, you are. I am celebrating my lucky escape! I succumbed to a bit of moon madness today on the beach—or should we call that sun madness, to be precise about the thing? For we should be precise about the thing, shouldn't we? I mean, a woman like you—who takes down her long blonde hair in front of a wounded, isolated, woman-starved veteran—wouldn't wish for it to be bruited about that she was the flighty sort who would trifle with a man's affections...now, would she?''

Elly rose, drawing her ivory cashmere shawl tightly about her damnably soft, silky shoulders. ''John,'' she said quietly, ''I think you should leave. We are, after all, unchaperoned once more, and I think you are a little the worse for drink.''

He poured another three fingers of brandy and tossed it off. ''Oh, a little the worse for drink, am I? And we all know how you feel about that, don't we, Miss Dalrymple? But just think—what it cost you in your father, you got back a hundredfold in the late Earl.''

''What do you care about the late Earl? I fail to understand your interest in the man. You seem to think I should be building a shrine to him or some such nonsense.''

He ignored her, as his tongue had taken control of his abused senses. He was feeling sorry for himself, the maligned, rightful Earl of Hythe, and sorry for his other self, the turned-down suitor, John Bates. As a matter of fact, he felt like the sorriest beast in nature.

Stung, he went on the attack. ''Of course you don't want me, madam. Try to fob me off with some far-radiddle about tainted blood, will you? You've got Leslie and his lovely money so firmly under your thumb that *you'd* be the insane one—to marry a penniless veteran and bail out of the deepest gravy boat in all England! The only taint you have is greed—and you have a bellyful of it. Well, let me tell you, madam, I shall go down on my knees this night and thank God that you don't want me, for I sure as hell don't want you!''

''You're drunk, and you don't know what you're saying,'' Elly told him, backing slowly toward the door. ''Once again, I must ask you to leave.''

''Leave? Leave my own—leave my own *true love?*'' he amended prudently, for he was not so angry nor so bosky that he was going to give the game away now. Oh, no. He was going to play out the whole string now—right to the very end. And she, Elinor Dalrymple, was going to dance to his tune.

Slamming the snifter down on the sideboard, he crossed the room so swiftly that Elly had no chance to react—to run. And before he had a moment to consider the real reason behind his actions, Alastair grabbed her by the shoulders and ground his mouth against hers in a kiss that was meant to show her all that she would be missing now that she had turned him down.

When the kiss was over, even though the sweet scent and soft touch of her mouth would haunt him for the rest of the evening—perhaps for the rest of his life—Alastair turned for the door.

''Oh, yes—about his business of having Leslie married off,'' he said, turning back to her with a wide sweep of his arm, as if just recalling something he had wanted to say, ''as far as I can tell, the only person besides the Biggses to have taken the man's fancy seems to be Hugo—and let me tell you, madam, I shall refuse the banns!''

CHAPTER FIVE

ELLY SPENT the majority of the next two days in a veritable frenzy of housekeeping, trying her utmost to banish the memory of that disastrous evening with John Bates from her mind. Mostly she tried to erase the memory of his kiss, which had set her heart to pounding even as she realized that his gesture had been meant as more of an insult than an expression of passion.

She had never been so angry, so embarrassed, so frustrated—or so hurt—in her entire life. Try as she might to convince herself that she had no feelings for the man other than suspicion, she knew she had been hoping against hope that in truth he had found her attractive.

But, as she had thought, he had been only toying with her, just as she had been toying with him. Yet, she knew after spending two long, almost sleepless nights considering the thing, she could still harbor the dream that he was now feeling just as confused and letdown as she was at their angry parting.

How had she ever gotten herself involved in such a stupid, convoluted project?

"It all started with Lieutenant Fishbourne," she reminded herself rationally as she laid cedar chips in the drawers in Leslie's chamber. "If he hadn't filled my head with all those tales of spies and smugglers, I wouldn't have given John Bates's appearance at Seashadow a second thought."

A mental picture of the blonde, colorless Jason Fishbourne as he had sat in Seashadow's drawing room, pompously and endlessly expounding on the history of the area, filled her mind. "As a matter of fact, I believe I am quite out of charity with the man. To add to his sins, the Lieutenant is also the most *boring* man I have ever met!"

Slamming the drawer shut on Leslie's flannels, Elly strode over to his bed and straightened the already pristine coverlet. "I'm not being fair," she admitted to the empty room. "I would have been suspicious of John Bates whether the Lieutenant had warned me against strangers or not. The man has intrigued me ever since I first laid eyes on him. His sudden appearance, his reluctance to talk about himself, his feigned limp, his seeming familiarity with Seashadow—they simply don't fit his explanation for being here."

She walked into the hallway, turning toward the narrow servants' stairs that led directly to the kitchens. "And then there's Hugo," she groused as her uncooperative brain persisted in tormenting her even as she tried to clear her mind of everything save the efficient running of Seashadow.

"Why would a man keep a brute like that, if it weren't for protection? Good Lord, the man is the perfect guard dog. He can't even speak—to give away John's secrets. And, while I am on the subject, why am *I* speaking out loud—and to myself? If Mrs. Biggs were to hear me, she'd probably want to immediately dose me with salts or something. I really must exercise more caution.''

As she entered the kitchens in the hope of finding something mundane to do to occupy her time, Elly stopped, sighed, and asked with controlled calm, ''Leslie? You aren't bothering Big George again, are you? And get down from that table this instant. Can't you see Little George is trying to chop carrots?''

Leslie obediently hopped down from his perch, his pencils and drawing tablet tumbling to the stone floor. ''Now look what you made me do, Elly,'' he complained pettishly—for he could be pettish when his concentration was interrupted.

''I didn't make you do anything, dearest,'' she returned wearily. ''I never could, more's the pity, and I'll thank you not to remind me of my failure. But, if you will, Leslie, please satisfy my curiosity even as you accept my apology. What were you doing perched on the table?''

Leslie grinned, mollified. ''There was a spider weaving his web inside one of the pots up there,'' he told her, pointing to the string of brightly shining copper pots hanging above the heavy wooden chopping table, ''and I had nearly captured his expression before you distracted me.''

''Of course. I knew it would be a simple explanation. Little Georgie,'' Elly ordered sternly, for she was sorry she had asked the question, as she was in no mood to listen to her brother's foolishness, ''either dispatch the spider to its reward or remove it to some other, less dangerous place. I definitely do not wish to see its 'expression' looking up at me from my plate at luncheon.''

"Yes, ma'am, right away, ma'am," Little Georgie spluttered, taking down the pot and heading for the door to the kitchen garden.

Leslie followed after him, his sketch pad clutched to his thin chest, his pencils escaping his grasp to make a drunken path from table to door, muttering, "I'll have to begin all over, you know. He won't look pensive anymore. He'll look terrified—or angry." As he turned to retrieve a single pencil, he pulled a face behind his sister's back.

"And don't stick out your tongue, Leslie," Elly cautioned without turning away from the dry sink she was inspecting for signs of mold. "You're too old for that sort of nonsense, you know."

"Yes, Elly—sorry," Leslie mumbled before bolting once more for the door.

Elly pinched the bridge of her nose between her fingers, knowing she would have to seek her brother out later and apologize to him. Having learned long ago that she could not change him, make him more responsible, she had vowed that she would do her best never to lose patience with him.

It was all John Bates's fault, she decided as her lips clamped into a tight, straight line. If her brain weren't so crammed full with thoughts of him, she wouldn't be so liable to snap off everyone else's heads with her short temper.

"Would Master Bates be comin' ter dinner agin tonight, missy?" Mrs. Biggs asked, the large woman coming up behind her so silently that Elly nearly dropped the egg she had absently lifted from a wire basket containing two dozen eggs just brought in from the henhouse.

John Bates, again! Was she to be allowed no peace, no escape from the man? Carefully replacing the egg, she counted to ten, then turned slowly about to look at the housekeeper.

The woman was holding Baby Willie on one comfortably wide hip, and the child once again had both hands stuck in his mouth while a foot-long string of drool hung from his left elbow.

"I thought Rosie was minding Baby Willie while you oversaw Iris and Lily as they cleaned the silver," Elly remarked questioningly, sidestepping the issue of John Bates as she searched in her pockets for a handkerchief with which to wipe the cooing child's wet face.

"I sent Rosie ter her bed, Missy, as she was feelin' poorly," Mrs. Biggs answered, shifting Baby Willie to her other hip. "Could be measles."

"Measles!" Elly shrieked, rapidly reviewing her past to remember whether or not she and Leslie had ever had the measles. Yes, she'd had them, but she didn't think Leslie had. "Are you quite sure it's measles, Mrs. Biggs?" she asked, knowing that Leslie and Rosie had been skipping stones into the Channel together the other day. This was what came of having a gaggle of children in a house that should boast fully grown footmen and chambermaids and parlormaids— all of whom would most probably have already had the measles.

Mrs. Biggs shrugged. "I said it could be—mayhap it's nuthin' but somethin' she ate. She tossed her breakfast right back at me the minute she ate it. Besides, now that I think on it, Rose already had the measles."

"Then why did you say—oh, never mind. Please disregard the question," Elly said as mildly as she could, wondering why she continued to put up with the Biggses. After all, just because the late Earl had hired them was no reason for Leslie to keep the family on—even if he was enthralled by them.

Just as she was about to open her mouth and hint that the Biggses would have to find some way to staff the house and keep the younger children tucked away in their living quarters, Baby Willie stretched out his damp hands, grinned his babyish grin, and launched himself into Elly's arms.

"Baby Willie!" Mrs. Biggs scolded, grabbing at the child's ankles while Elly staggered beneath the sudden weight of Baby Willie's sturdy young body. "My, my, missy, would yer look at that. He sure has taken a likin' ter yer, hasn't he? My Baby Willie doesn't go ter just anybody, yer know."

Knowing that Baby Willie's affection might have something to do with the fact that she had begun slipping him sweets when no one was looking, Elly suffered the child's embrace in silence, feeling her traitorous heart melting away her resolve to remake Seashadow's staff into something less reminiscent of a well-run haven for drooling children.

"I'm flattered, Mrs. Biggs" was all Elly could say, taking Baby Willie fully into her arms. "As a matter of fact, now that I have him, would you mind if we took a stroll outside? I have been cooped up much too long in this fine weather."

"That you have," Mrs. Biggs seconded with an audible sigh, and Elly immediately got the feeling that the woman would be more than grateful to have her new mistress out from under her feet so that she could run Seashadow the way she wanted without any interference. "But about Mr. Bates, missy—"

Elly's temporarily lifted spirits plummeted at the mention of the man's name. "Mr. Bates again. What about Mr. Bates, Mrs. Biggs?"

"Will he be comin' ter dinner agin any time soon, d'yer think? Big George was thinkin' of fixin' his favorite—stuffed capon."

Baby Willie squealed aloud as Elly's arms closed a little too tightly around his pudgy middle. "His favorite, Mrs. Biggs? You don't say. How would you know that?"

The housekeeper fumbled with her apron for a moment, her blue eyes wide as saucers, then lifted her head and said brightly, "He told me so himself—just yesterday. He brought Hugo ter the kitchens ter see Baby Willie. Those two are getting' on like a house afire, missy."

Elly looked at the woman levelly. "Of course. I should have realized that," she answered, turning for the door. "No, Mr. Bates is not coming for dinner this evening. However, the Earl is also partial to stuffed capons, so they won't go to waste. I'll have Baby Willie back before luncheon, Mrs. Biggs. Please see that either Iris or Lily is available at that time to take him from me."

"Lily." Mrs. Biggs sniffed derisively as Elly turned to the door. "The smithy is visitin' down ter the stables, missy. We'll be lucky if we see that one afore dinner! Big George is goin' ter have ter go husband-huntin' for that one soon, afore he has to do it with his cleaver ter hand."

For the next hour, as she and Baby Willie played on the sand, Elly considered all the ways Mrs. Biggs could have known that John Bates's favorite dish was stuffed capons—for as surely as she knew she was beginning to fall in love with the odious man, she was just as certain that the housekeeper had been lying to her about his visit to the kitchens.

There were only two answers.

One was that John Bates and the Biggses had known each other a lot longer than they had let on, proving that John was in the area for some reason other than to recuperate from some vague war wound—most probably making himself at home at Seashadow until she and Leslie had arrived, and then removing himself to the nearby cottage.

But why would he have been living at Seashadow? Were the Biggses also smugglers—or spies? No, she couldn't picture the Biggses in either role. After all, what would they do with the children?

That left but one alternative. John Bates could be working for the government, in much the same way the so-boring Lieutenant Fishbourne was. Yet, if he was, why didn't the Lieutenant know about him? And why would he feel he had to keep his true reason for being at Seashadow a secret from the Earl and his sister?

She finally concluded, much as it pained her, that she was going to have to swallow her pride, bury her traitorous personal feelings for the man, and continue to see John Bates, if only to satisfy her curiosity.

Their argument of the other evening would make it very difficult, as would her growing knowledge that she was becoming more than a little fond of the man.

''For all the good that will do me,'' she told a giggling Baby Willie as she tickled his bare stomach. ''I hurt him badly when I turned him down—even if we both knew he hadn't really meant to court me—and I shall have his injured sensibilities to deal with before I have any chance of learning his secrets.''

Walking down to the water's edge so that she and Willie could gather shells, she stopped in her tracks, suddenly realizing that there was a third, hitherto unthought-of possibility—another answer to why John Bates was so familiar with Seashadow.

But that other answer was too ridiculous, too insanely ludicrous, too farfetched, for her to even consider. Wasn't it?

ALASTAIR WATCHED as Elly, Baby Willie held high in her arms, ran toward the incoming waves, then retreated as they chased her, the pair's delighted giggles floating upward on the air to where he stood.

He felt abandoned, lonely, and envious of a small child who could make Elly laugh, while all he could seem to do was make her angry—and suspicious.

He reached a hand into his pocket, to crush the missive from Wiggins that had arrived only that morning. The Dalrymples were the genuine heirs—Wiggins would stake his reputation on it. The Captain had had his sources in London check with the Hythe solicitors, and everything was in order, although the solicitors had been amazed when they had stumbled over the existence of the last of the Dalrymple family. If Alastair Lowell were to have actually perished at sea, his very distant cousin, Leslie Dalrymple, would truly be the Earl of Hythe.

"I always knew it," Alastair said aloud, happy no one could hear his blatant, face-saving lie.

What a fool he had been! Had he actually believed that Elinor Dalrymple could be a money-mad impostor, or a smuggler, or even a traitor to her country? Had he actually convinced himself that—if she was a legitimate relative—she would have stooped to killing him in order to set her brother up as Earl?

Yes. Yes, damn his eyes, he had.

But he hadn't needed Wiggins's missive explaining how the Lowell solicitors had had to track down Leslie and Elly and convince them of the rightness of their claim to the title to straighten him out.

He had known the truth from the moment he'd kissed her—possibly even from the moment she'd taken down her hair on the beach and smiled up at him.

Fighting down the urge to join her on the beach and apologize to her—on his knees if necessary—Alastair turned away from the shore and headed for Seashadow, intent on meeting with Leslie, barely noticing as Hugo stepped out from behind a tree to follow him.

At least Leslie liked him—or Alastair would like to think so. Perhaps through the brother he could find a way back to the sister.

"The sister who—thanks to my stupidity—believes that I am either a spy, a smuggler, or worse," he told himself as he passed by the small stable and waved to Harry Biggs—who seemed to be yelling at the man-hungry Lily, while she most happily had her back turned to him. "Wiggins's letter says that his man—Fishbait, or whatever his name is—called on Elly to warn her of smugglers and spies using Seashadow's beaches. Now everything is falling into place. The dratted woman thinks I'm a spy—me! the Earl of Hythe!—and she's out to single-handedly catch me at it! Lord, I think I love that woman!''

"*Aaaarrggh! Aaah!*"

"*What?*" Alastair exclaimed, nearly jumping out of his skin as he whirled about to see the giant lumbering along three paces behind him, a grin as wide as a cavern splitting his face. "Christ on a crutch, man, don't ever sneak up on me like that again! How can anything so big move so quietly? And why are you looking at me like that? Oh," he said, shamefaced, remembering what he had just confessed to the air, "you heard me, my friend, didn't you?"

The giant nodded vigorously, clasping his hamlike hands to his chest and closing his eyes, as if in ecstasy.

Alastair's mouth began to twitch as a grin threatened to overtake him. "Evil as this sounds, my friend, this is one time I am actually glad your tongue suffered that little accident. I don't think I could hear your sentiments on the subject without becoming completely unmanned. I'm having enough difficulty reconciling myself to my unexpected mad-for-love state as it is.''

"*Gluugg, gluugg,*" Hugo responded, patting Alastair's shoulder with one large paw, as if to tell him he understood the mixed feelings of a man who has just discovered that he has met his match, and his carefree bachelorhood was all but behind him.

As the pair crossed the rolled and scythed lawns that ran like a green lake from the raised porch surrounding the rear of Seashadow, Hugo split away from Alastair to head in the direction of the kitchens, his hand gestures conveying to his friend that he was on the hunt for a handout from Big George.

"If he has strawberry tarts, be sure to snaffle one for me as well," Alastair called after him as he mounted the stone steps to the wide flagstone porch and walked toward the French doors that stood open to the billiards room.

"Knock, knock! Is anyone home?" he called out cheerily as he entered the room, then ejaculated in sudden horror, "*Good God!* What in blazes happened in here? It looks like a Tothill tavern after a brawl. And what's that god-awful smell?"

There was a slight rustling in one corner of the jumbled room before Leslie Dalrymple's face rose above the back of Alastair's favorite leather sofa, and pulling an unfolded sheet of newspaper from its resting place atop his head, he exclaimed, "John! I thought I heard someone call. I was just meditating—contemplating my next work. This is my studio, you understand."

Alastair took another three steps into the room, scarcely recognizing it for what it had been when he had been the Earl—a snug retreat where a man could drink or play billiards with his chums without danger of being interrupted. "Where's the billiard table, Leslie?" he asked quietly, not knowing whether he felt closer to mayhem or to tears.

"The billiards table?" Leslie repeated blankly, uncurling his skinny frame and rising to look about the room inquiringly. "Oh, of course. You must mean this thing," he said, walking across the debris-strewn carpet to point to a large rectangular object covered end to end with paint pots, sketch pads, one half (the bottom half) of a suit of armor, glass jars filled with a variety of insects, several pieces of fruit in various stages of decay—which accounted for the sickly sweet odor Alastair had noticed—and a cannonball-sized lump that must have been Leslie's string collection. "Isn't it a perfectly wonderful worktable? It has these lovely deep, knitted pockets in all the corners—see? I use them to hold my best brushes."

"That—that's my—that's the billiards table?" Alastair squeaked, feeling physically ill as he belatedly recognized the piece of furniture for what it was. He also recognized several of the paint and brush pots— for they were a small portion of his very select, very rare china collection. "Oh, I've got to put a stop to this madness once and for all, before this chucklehead lays ruin to the whole place!"

"What's that you say, John?" Leslie asked, for he had been busily wadding a piece of newspaper before looking at it, as if trying to decide what to do with it, shrugging, and throwing it to the floor to join a half dozen others just like it. "Uh-oh. You have that same pinched look Elly gets every time she comes in here. Don't you like my studio?"

"No, Leslie," Alastair bit out from between clenched teeth. "As a matter of fact, I don't think I do."

Leslie shrugged once more. "Well, no matter. I do." He spread his arms and turned about slowly, as if inviting inspection of his rumpled person as an alternative. "Maybe you'll like m'suit? It just came from the city. Elly has the dressing of me, you understand, ever since I ordered three yellow and black waistcoats from a man who came through our village

a few years ago—she said I looked like an underfed
bumblebee.''

Alastair wasn't listening. He was too busy looking
at the once flawless green felt tabletop that was now
damaged beyond repair, beyond any hope of redemption. He lifted a Sèvres vase, trying to chip away some
of the hardened paint with his thumbnail before putting it down very carefully—so that he wouldn't give
in to the temptation to throw the thing at Leslie's head.

"Your sister allows this—this desecration?" he
asked at last, lifting a stuffed owl from one of the
chairs and sitting himself down before he fell down.
"I thought Mrs. Biggs had assured me—had told me
Elly was a stickler for good housekeeping."

Leslie nodded vigorously. "Oh, she is, she is. Elly's
a real crackerjack. But I found the key, you understand, so I can keep her locked out most of the time.
She'd have a spasm if she could see how my studio
looks right now. You won't tell her, will you, John?
We can keep it our secret."

Alastair was about to point out that locking the door
to the rest of the house didn't mean much when one
left the doors to the porch wide open for anyone to
enter, but he didn't think he was up to the task. Instead, he said, "I promise, Leslie. It will be our secret."

"You! What are you doing here?"

Alastair turned to see Elly standing in the doorway,
Baby Willie in her arms, the hem of her pink gown
wet with sand, her tiny face a study in confused hos-
tility.

He wanted to run to her, to kiss her, to clasp her
hard against his chest forever—for she looked so dear,

so appealing, with her glorious hair having escaped its pins to tumble over her shoulders.

Not only that, but after spending so much time with only the wordless Hugo, the eccentric Leslie, and the war-mad Wiggins for company, he suddenly felt her to be the only sane person left in the world save himself—and he feared that he was fast losing his grip on that sanity.

He couldn't tell her any of this, of course—at least, not until he revealed who he really was. Besides, his tender feelings for her might just be a temporary aberration—brought on by his circumstances, the ruined felt, the paint pots, or the pickled insects—although he seriously doubted it. To cover his own confusion, he leapt to his feet, to respond to her rather rude greeting.

"Yes, yes, it is he!" he shouted, resorting to humor, flinging his arms dramatically wide. "Barricade the doors—the windows! That terrible John is back!" Then he sat at his ease, placed one elbow on the arm of the chair and his chin in his palm, smiled, waggled his eyebrows mischievously, and proclaimed gaily, "And how are you this fine afternoon, Miss Dalrymple? Feeling especially maternal today, are you?" He turned to Leslie. "What do you think, my friend? Is that a picture to inspire your muse, or isn't it?"

Elly advanced into the room to stand beside the chair and stare down at him. "Are you all right?" she asked, and he thought he heard a trace of real concern in her voice.

No, he wasn't. He had never felt less "right" in his life. But he was not about to tell Elinor Dalrymple that! Instead, he grinned up at her, knowing he should

be on his feet while she was standing, but doggedly
refusing to rise. "I am enjoying my usual good
health—having fully recovered from my wounds—but
thank you *so* much for asking, Miss Dalrymple."

He didn't add that he could tell even more precisely
that he was in his usual good health because he felt
so much better today than he had all the previous day,
when he had been nursing a bruising hangover from
the brandy he'd imbibed the last time the two of them
had met.

She looked down at him for a long time—a lifetime
during which Alastair thought of and discarded a
dozen ways to tell her who he really was, knowing the
truth had to be told while at the same time understanding that she would be devastated to learn that she and
her brother were once more penniless.

Just as he thought he would have to either confess
his identity or burst, Elly looked away to address her
brother. "I shall deliver Baby Willie to the kitchens
and take something to settle my stomach—for I believe the smell in here must be what is making it
queasy—before returning here with Iris in order to attempt to make some sense of this chaos you have created, Leslie. I suggest you walk on the beach while
we work, as I refuse to fight with you over the prac-
ticality of disposing of most of this mess."

Both men watched as Elly left through the French
doors, then Leslie groaned aloud. "Elly's taken one
of her pets again. This isn't the first time I've given
her the stomachache—although why she should be so
upset, I'll never understand, as it is *my* studio and I
never asked her to live in it. She'll destroy everything,
you know, John, trying to put it in order. I really

thought she would leave me alone in this studio—as she doesn't care a whit for billiards, and the light is quite good—but Elly needs must put everything to order. I think it's a sickness.''

"She is a good housekeeper, then?'' Alastair asked, glad to hear it from another source. He couldn't love a poor housekeeper.

"Good? She's top o' the trees when it comes to housekeeping. She has even hung a list of rules in the kitchens. Mrs. Biggs told me about it, but that dear lady only thinks it's funny.''

Alastair nodded, not surprised to hear of Mrs. Biggs's easy acceptance of the list—as he full well knew that none of the Biggses could read more than their own names. "Your sister would have been horrified to see how the previous Earl used this place early in his salad days—not that it wasn't always kept scrupulously clean, for the Earl too loved order in his everyday life. But, if what I heard in the village the other day is true, the man wasn't above riding his favorite horse straight up the steps and into the drawing room one night when he was particularly full of frisk.''

"You don't say!'' Leslie commented, his smile lighting his formerly wan features. "I rather like that. You know, John, I've just had the happy notion that it might behoove me to rethink attempting an oil rendering of the man—for I do owe him a lot. If he hadn't died, I don't know where Elly and I would be now. Do you think there's a likeness of him about somewhere? This may be the family seat, but it isn't the largest Lowell estate and doesn't have a portrait gallery. But no, I suppose I shouldn't consider it, knowing how Elly feels about the man.''

Alastair was past caring whether or not Leslie managed to dig up a likeness of him somewhere in Seashadow. He was past trying to satisfy his curiosity by searching the Lowell family histories for traces of Dalrymples—for he believed Wiggins's information that Elly and Leslie were legitimate.

Mostly he was past continuing this stupid, ill-conceived deception. The moment, the very moment, he had awakened in Hugo's hovel, he should have summoned his solicitors and informed them of his lucky escape, and all the misunderstandings, all the suspicions, all the ridiculous fencing between Elly and himself, could have been avoided.

''Because I would never have met her!'' Alastair whispered hoarsely, the impact of his mental revelations succeeding in banishing any lingering remains of caution, any reticence keeping him from doing what he had come to Seashadow today to do—tell Elly the truth. ''My God,'' he exclaimed, forgetting he had an audience, ''what a tragedy that would have been! I have to go to her, at once!''

Leslie laid a hand on Alastair's arm, sympathetic but completely misunderstanding. ''Oh, I am sorry, John. Don't take on so, though it's dashed good of you to want to come to my defense. It's not a tragedy—remember, it's only a picture. What does it matter if Elly dislikes it?''

''What?'' Alastair asked uncomprehendingly. He looked down at the younger man—the man who thought he was the Fifteenth Earl of Hythe—and got an idea. He wouldn't go directly to Elly. He'd tell

Leslie first, assure him that everything would be fine—considering that the Fourteenth Earl wished to marry his sister—and then the two of them would go to Elly together. That way, Alastair might just have a chance to explain everything without being tossed out of his own home on his ear!

"Leslie," Alastair crooned, putting his arm around the man's shoulders, "walk with me on the porch awhile, will you? I have something to tell you, and I'd rather do it away from the smell of overripe fruit."

"Elly said to walk on the beach," Leslie pointed out, then grinned. "Not that I don't like the beach, you understand. Both Elly and I had never seen the sea until we came to Seashadow. As a matter of fact, that's why we came here first, rather than to any of the other estates. But I'm the Earl, aren't I? I can do what I want—even if I want to commission another three yellow and black waistcoats. It has taken me some time to get the hang of it, John, but I have to own it—I do enjoy being an Earl."

"I rather wished you hadn't shared that particular revelation with me, Leslie, old son," Alastair said, wincing.

Leslie, as usual ignoring all but his own feelings, slipped an arm about Alastair's waist. "Yes, John, let us walk on the porch," he agreed happily as the two of them stepped out onto the flagstones.

Ping! The sudden sound of metal hitting brick, following hard on the muffled sound of a distant shot, had Alastair unceremoniously throwing Leslie and himself forward onto the flagstones. He lay there behind the low stone wall lining the edge of the porch, his head raised slightly as he searched the tree line for a hint of a gun barrel glinting in the sunlight, but he didn't see anything.

After a moment he turned his body about to look at the mellow pink brick that was head-high next to the open doorway. Yes, there was a raw scar in the mortar and—he saw a moment later—a ball embedded in the wall.

"What—what happened?" Leslie croaked at last, rubbing at his bruised shoulder. "Was that a shot, John?"

"It was," Alastair answered, helping Leslie to his feet and back into the billiards room, "but I don't think there will be another one."

"No, there never has been before," Leslie answered absently, brushing off his pants.

Alastair, who still had his eyes trained on the trees, whirled about to face Leslie. No, it was impossible! It didn't make any sense. *He* had been the one targeted for murder, hadn't he? If somehow someone had discovered that Hugo had saved him, it stood to reason that the bullet had been another attempt, meant for him. It was the only thing that made sense. "Before?" he questioned softly. "What do you mean, Leslie? Has this happened before?"

Leslie nodded. "You won't tell Elly about this, will you, John? Elly won't let me out of her sight if she hears about it. After all, it's only stray bullets from hunters, or poachers, isn't it? Just like the toadstools were an accident—and the rock that fell near me on the beach. But you know women—she'll probably start reading all sorts of nonsense into a few coincidences if you get upset now too. Elly does that sort of thing most especially well."

Alastair's head was reeling. He had been concentrating for so long on believing the Dalrymples to be guilty that he had refused to believe Wiggins's theory that someone—either spies or smugglers or both—had wanted the Earl out of the way so that they had free access to Seashadow.

As he had only changed his mind about the Dalrymples this morning, he had yet to think up another theory as to who could be behind his near drowning. Now it looked as if Geoffrey Wiggins had been right all along.

Alastair was supposed to be dead. Perhaps—as he had believed himself—the murderers had thought the title would revert to the crown once the last Earl of Hythe was dead—leaving Seashadow to be run by a skeleton staff, its beaches fair game to anyone who wished to set up housekeeping there. Who was to stop them—the Biggses? Hardly.

But Alastair hadn't been the end of the line. There had been Leslie, and Elly, both of them walked the beach daily.

And now the murderers were after Leslie!

Alastair opened his mouth to tell Leslie what he thought, caught a glimpse of the shambles that was once his billiards table, and thought better of it. It would be like talking to the wind to even attempt to explain this convoluted intrigue to Leslie Dalrymple.

He would just have to assign Hugo to guard the man until he could lay everything out in front of Elly, call in Wiggins, who was still in London trying to tie things up at that end, and locate the person or persons who were trying to eradicate the residents of Seashadow!

Ordering Leslie—who was already most happily engaged in adding a coat of paint to a canvas boasting the rendering of a single blade of grass—to stay put until Hugo could join him, Alastair headed for the kitchens, hoping to locate Elly.

"Missy's up in her room, your lordship," Mrs. Biggs told him a few moments later, clucking her tongue. "I think she's come down with what Rosie's got—or at least she came inter the kitchens lookin' as green as Rosie did a while ago, though Rosie's settin' up and sippin' soup now, tryin' her best ter fill up her empty belly. It comes on sudden, and leaves just as quick. I suppose I'll have 'em all down with it afore too long. Do you want me to send Iris upstairs ter ask Missy ter come down?"

Alastair rubbed a weary hand across his forehead. His confession—as well as his suspicion that her brother's life was in danger—would have to wait for another day. "No, Billie, don't disturb her. Just have Harry get some of the farm laborers to help him stand guard all around Seashadow tonight, and send someone to fetch me tomorrow as soon as Miss Dalrymple is up to seeing visitors. Hugo will be staying with Mr. Dalrymple."

"Is somethin' goin' on, yer lordship?" Mrs. Biggs asked. "Somethin's goin' on, ain't it? Are we goin' ter be able ter stop this playactin' soon?"

"Soon, Billie, very soon," Alastair assured her, scooping up two still warm strawberry tarts as he headed for the door, before stopping to tell the woman mournfully, "Believe me, I like this even less than you. Have you seen what he's done to my billiards room, Billie?"

''It's a cryin' shame, your lordship,'' the house-keeper commiserated, shaking her head. ''But yer'll set it all ter rights soon, yer lordship, and so say we all.''

Alastair's shoulders shook in wry mirth as he walked back out through the kitchen garden. ''Poor Billie,'' he said aloud. ''Wait until she finds out that Leslie Dalrymple is to become a permanent fixture at Seashadow. The whole lot of them will probably hand in their notices.''

CHAPTER SIX

ELLY STARED INTO the mirror in the drawing room, a hand to her cheek, appalled at the sight of the white face that looked back at her.

"Good afternoon, Miss Dalrymple."

She whirled about—the quick movement reminding her of the still-not-quite-settled state of her stomach—to see Lieutenant Jason Fishbourne standing beside the open doors leading from the patio.

"Lieu-Lieutenant!" she exclaimed unsteadily, before her rising temper hardened her tone. How did he walk in on her, unannounced? "Have you lost your way? The front door—and the knocker—are on quite the opposite side of the house."

The man appeared impervious to insult. He bowed deeply from the waist, saying only, "We have pressing matters to discuss, madam, *privately,*" before walking more fully into the room.

"We do? *Indeed?*" Elly countered, wondering if all men were so rude, or if blonde men, like John Bates and the Lieutenant—and even her beloved brother Leslie—had some taint in their blood that predisposed them to riding roughshod over the formalities. "And what would those matters be, sir?"

She walked over to the settee, motioning for the Lieutenant to sit across from her, and sat down, for her legs still weren't too steady twenty-four hours after her brief but violent relationship with whatever stomach upset was fast laying low nearly every Biggs at Seashadow. Mrs. Biggs, Big and Little Georgie, Iris, Harry, and even Baby Willie had all fallen victim to the same illness during the night—which undoubtedly had made it easier for Fishbourne to make his way into the house unchallenged.

She watched as the Lieutenant sat back at his ease, crossing one long leg over the other. "You have a guest on the estate, madam, I believe?" he asked without further preamble. "One Mr. John Bates?"

Elly's heart began pounding hurtfully in her chest. "I do," she answered, knowing her chin was tilting at an aggressive angle. "Does that present a problem to you, Lieutenant?"

Fishbourne searched in his pocket for a small copybook, holding it in front of him as he read what was written there. "Name, John Bates. Occupation, retired soldier in His Majesty's service. Personal history, none. Companion, a hulking deaf and dumb brute named Hugo."

"Only dumb," Elly corrected, feeling her hackles beginning to rise anew. "Although I must say I dislike that description intensely, as it implies that Hugo is stupid as well as speechless. Nothing could be further from the truth. As a matter of fact, Hugo's intelligent action saved my brother from a nasty fall just the other day."

The Lieutenant looked up from the pages of the copybook, directed a level, assessing stare at Elly, and then returned his eyes to the page. "I stand corrected, Miss Dalrymple. I shall, of course, adjust my notes accordingly once I am back at headquarters. Dumb, but not deaf. Now, if I might proceed?''

Doubting that she could stop him without resorting to physical violence, Elly motioned for the man to continue.

''The aforementioned Mr. Bates,'' Fishbourne went on, still consulting his notes, ''is a stranger to the area who somehow came into possession of a cottage on this estate for an indefinite term—paying no rent, by the way—through application to the Fourteenth Earl, your brother's predecessor.''

''Obviously a patriotic act of thanks to a man who had been injured fighting Napoleon,'' Elly said wearily, for it appeared the man was going to prolong his introduction into whatever matters he felt they had to ''discuss.''

''Alastair Lowell—*patriotic?* Surely, Miss Dalrymple, you jest. Yes, of course you do. I am much amused.'' As if to prove his amusement, Lieutenant Fishbourne laughed aloud, a short, barklike laugh that had the hairs on the back of Elly's neck standing at attention. ''The man was a useless wastrel, as I believe you yourself said.''

Whether it was because of her growing dislike for the Lieutenant or due to her own feelings of vulnerability about her initial opinion of the late Earl, Elly heard herself springing to the dead man's defense.

''I have been reading some of the late Earl's private papers, sir,'' she said, her voice cool, ''and I believe you to be in error. He was very active in Parliament on behalf of our soldiers in the field. As the last of his line—or so his solicitors have told me the man believed—and without issue, he had every reason not to endanger the Hythe succession by crossing the Channel to spill his blood on foreign soil. Someone, my dear Lieutenant, had to stay behind to help run the country. Have you, Lieutenant,'' she ended, hoping to change the subject, for she felt curiously uncomfortable in the role of defender of Alastair Lowell, ''served anywhere other than along the relative safety of these well-defended shores?''

His cold, faded green eyes raked her from head to foot as Elly mentally added the term ''dangerous'' to those she had already assigned to the man: pompous, boring, and rude. ''That is not germane, Miss Dalrymple,'' was all he answered as she involuntarily squirmed in her seat. ''We seem to have digressed. We were, I believe, discussing Mr. John Bates.''

''What about him?'' Elly asked pugnaciously, for ill as she still felt, she knew she was about to order this insufferable martinet out of her house.

The Lieutenant referred once more to his notes, tempting Elly to snatch the copybook from his hands and rip the offensive thing to shreds. ''The man is not what he appears, Miss Dalrymple. There is no record of a John Bates serving anywhere in His Majesty's army, in any capacity.''

Elly shrugged, hopefully appearing to be unimpressed by the Lieutenant's shattering news. ''So? Perhaps he served in His Majesty's navy. I think your information is incomplete.''

Fishbourne smiled at her. ''He said he had served in the army, Miss Dalrymple. I saw no reason to investigate further.''

Anxious not to draw out the interview, which was becoming increasingly painful to endure, Elly asked,

"Have you confronted Mr. Bates with your findings, Lieutenant?"

He ignored her question, his attention once more on his copious notes. "You—and your brother the Earl, of course—have been seen conversing with this Mr. John Bates, and he has partaken of his meals at Seashadow on several occasions."

"Two occasions, Lieutenant," Elly inserted through clenched teeth. Yes, she would definitely like to rip up that copybook—and stuff the pieces one by one down Fishbourne's throat. "I hadn't known that my brother and I were under surveillance, sir."

"No one is totally above suspicion, Miss Dalrymple, when the safety of our beloved country is at stake," Fishbourne informed her authoritatively, snapping the copybook shut at last. "Not that I believe you and the Earl could possibly be involved in any traitorous activity."

"How terribly condescending of you, Lieutenant," Elly purred with heavy sarcasm, rising to cross over to the bellpull, knowing that none of the Biggses were in any condition to come to her rescue.

Fishbourne rose as well, tucking the copybook back inside the jacket of his uniform. "My question, madam, is simply this: Why, when you said you would do all in your power to help your government, did you not report the existence of Mr. John Bates to me as soon as you discovered his presence on Seashadow property?"

It was a good question, Elly knew, and one she had racked her brain to answer on more than one occasion. After all, she had promised to report any suspicious person or persons, hadn't she?

Lieutenant Fishbourne considered John Bates to be suspicious, and he didn't even know about either the feigned limp or John's disquieting familiarity with Seashadow.

She opened her mouth to tell the man these things, then closed it again. She wasn't going to reveal her own discoveries about John Bates. She had never really planned to tell him—not deep in her heart of hearts. She was going to be stupid and foolish and protect John Bates from Lieutenant Fishbourne—behaving just like any at-her-last-prayers spinster who needs desperately to believe every man who so much as compliments her is in love with her.

She tugged once more on the bellpull, hoping her brother—whom she had last seen in the kitchens, creating some muddy-looking concoction he called "prunes and prisms gruel" for his luncheon—would come to her rescue. Where was Leslie when she needed him? Silly question. Where had he *ever* been when she needed him—nowhere to be found!

"Miss Dalrymple?" The Lieutenant had somehow come up beside her, and his voice made her flinch. "I sense some discomfort in your manner. He hasn't threatened you, this John Bates, has he?"

Of course John had threatened her. He threatened her peace, her supposedly well-ordered life, her traitorous heart that she had believed would always belong to Robert. She turned to face the Lieutenant, her smile as brilliant as she could make it. Elly closed her eyes, watching her figurative bridges burning into ashes behind her eyelids. "Threatened me, Lieutenant?" she repeated, then giggled. Lord, how she abhorred giggles! "Why, sir, I don't think so—unless you consider a proposal of marriage a threat."

Fishbourne took a single step back. "He—he proposed *marriage?*"

Well, Elly thought meanly, the man didn't have to sound so surprised. She knew she wasn't looking her best—what with her face still pinched from being ill and her hair pulled so unattractively atop her head— but he didn't have to make it seem as if John would have to be the most desperate, or least discriminating, creature on earth to have proposed to her.

Her chin lifted. "And what do you *think* he proposed, sirrah!" she asked archly. "I think, Lieutenant, that you overreach yourself."

For once she seemed to have penetrated Lieutenant Fishbourne's thick hide. "I—I didn't mean to infer— that is, I certainly was not implying that—"

Elly took his arm and steered him toward the door. "Of course you didn't, my dear Lieutenant," she said soothingly. "Just as I may have overreacted to your questions about my dearest John. You do understand how shocked I was to hear that you thought my betrothed could ever be involved with anything nefarious."

"Still," the Lieutenant persisted as Elly led him through the foyer, "I think I should stop by the cottage to meet your fiancé. Perhaps he has seen something unusual in the area?"

No! He couldn't see John—at least not until she could see him herself and tell him what she had just done! Giggling girlishly again, and hating herself twice as much for it, Elly trilled, "Oh, pray do not trouble yourself, Lieutenant. Mr. Bates has gone to visit his doctor somewhere or other today, and will not be back in his cottage until very late this evening. Perhaps you will accept an invitation to dine with all of us tomorrow night—giving me, *um,* giving my fiancé, that is, time to recuperate from his trip?''

Elly stood at the open front door, watching as the Lieutenant strode away, willing her pulse to return to its usual slow, steady beat. Now what had she done? Wasn't it bad enough that she had protected John Bates from the law? Had she really been forced to claim him as her fiancé as well? Now she had no choice but to go to John as soon as possible and convince him that her lies had been in his own best interests.

''Ah, there you are, Elly. I've been looking high and low for you. Now, let me think, what was it that I wanted?''

''Leslie.'' Elly turned about, letting the door slam behind her. ''Where have you been? I was summoning you with the bellpull.''

Leslie slapped his forehead with the palm of one hand. ''So *that's* what that infernal ringing was that I heard in the kitchen. And it's also why I don't remember why I wanted to see you. I never did want to see you. *You* wanted to see *me.* Don't do that, dearest Elly, please; you frightened me for a minute. I thought I was being more scatterbrained than usual. What did you want?''

Elly shook her head in defeat. ''Nothing, now. Leslie, I must go out for a while. Oh, Hugo,'' she said as the giant came into the foyer, a half-eaten apple in one large paw. ''What are you doing here? Never mind,

I'm happy to see you. Tell me, please, is your master at home?''

Hugo nodded, taking another bite of apple as Leslie commented, ''John? What do you care where he is, Elly? Just the other day you told me you were tired of him forever kicking his heels upon our doorstep. Said you wouldn't trust him across the street, too, if I remember it correctly—that and wishing him in Jericho a time or two. What do you want to see him about, Elly? Surely you aren't going to throw him out of the cottage? I shouldn't like that above half, Elly, truly I shouldn't.''

''The selectivity of your memory, my dearest brother,'' Elly returned in resignation, ''never ceases to astound me. No, I am not about to evict John from the cottage. I merely have some small matters to discuss with him,'' she told them, picking up her bonnet from a table near the door. ''Leslie, you and Hugo stay here in case the Biggses need you for anything.''

Leslie immediately looked crestfallen. ''They don't want me, Elly,'' he told her sadly. ''I took Mrs. Biggs some of my prunes and prisms gruel and she threw it out the window—bowl and all. Sick people aren't always nice, you know.''

''Yes, dearest,'' Elly answered vaguely, her mind concentrating on how she was going to tell John Bates that she had announced their ''engagement'' to Lieutenant Fishbourne. Even worse, she was going to have to confront him with her latest conclusion—the one that, if correct, would most probably put a period to their entire association. She opened the door and stepped out into the bright sunshine, feeling like a prisoner walking to the gibbet. ''I shan't be long.''

THE MANTEL CLOCK chimed out the hour of two, and still Harry hadn't come to tell him that Elly was up to seeing visitors. Alastair continued to pace the carpet in the overcrowded main room of the comfortable, quaint cottage, trying to wish the hours away until he could stand before her at Seashadow and tell her the truth.

A knock at the front door interrupted his thoughts and he nearly ran in his haste to open it, only to find the object of his thoughts standing on the smooth stone doorstep.

He looked around quickly, just to see if she was alone, then pulled her unceremoniously inside the cottage, slamming the door behind them. "What in blue blazes is the matter with Harry? How could he have let you out by yourself at a time like this? And here I always thought he was the smart one."

Disengaging her elbow from his grip, Elly walked toward the oak settle, stripping off her bonnet as she sat down. "Harry?" she asked, fiddling with the strings of her bonnet. "What has Harry to say to anything? And why are you acting as if I shouldn't be seen coming into your cottage? Not that I should be, but as no one was about to chaperone me, and this cottage is quite isolated, I didn't think it would matter. We've been alone before, John, if you'll recall."

She was as nervous as a Christmas goose around a chopping block, Alastair decided as he walked across the room to sit on the oak settle that faced hers. Had she heard something? Had she sensed some change in the atmosphere? Had there been another attempt on Leslie's life? "What are you doing here, Elly? I was planning to visit you at Seashadow once you were feeling better. You are feeling better, aren't you?'' he asked, eyeing her pale face intently.

''Doing here?'' she answered before biting her lip as she looked around the room that was crowded with so much furniture that Alastair had been forced to banish Hugo from its confines for fear he would forget himself, turn around too quickly, and demolish something. ''And I'm just fine, thank you, although most of the Biggses are now suffering from the same complaint. My, what a lovely corner cupboard that is, John. I do believe it is mahogany. There is quite a wealth of furniture in here, isn't there? You are comfortable here, I trust? I imagine I should have stopped by sooner, to be sure you were. How many rooms are there in the cottage, all together, that is?''

Something was wrong. Elly was babbling, and she wasn't the sort of women who babbled. ''Four, and yes, I am very comfortable, although the ceiling could be a foot higher for Hugo. Would you now like to discuss the weather—which continues to be very fine—or would you like to tell me what really brought you here before you wad that poor ribbon up past all saving?''

He watched as she looked down to see the havoc her nervously twitching hands had wrought on her bonnet strings, smiling as she deliberately smoothed the ribbons and laid the bonnet to one side. ''John, can we talk with the buttons off?'' she asked, staring straight up at him, her eyes wide with apprehension.

Finally! He was beginning to think he was going to have to shake Elly's news out of her. Alastair crossed his legs, leaning back against the settle. ''I certainly don't see why we shouldn't, my dear. We certainly haven't skirted around each other's sensibilities up to now, have we? What do you want to talk about?''

She took a deep breath, then said, ''Lieutenant Jason Fishbourne!''

Alastair sat forward, his attention caught. He could have thought of a half dozen subjects she might wish to discuss—perhaps an even dozen. But Lieutenant Jason Fishbourne? *''Who?''*

''Lieutenant Fishbourne is investigating smuggling and spying that may be taking place right here at Seashadow. Then you don't know him,'' Elly said, as if convincing herself. ''Well, he knows you. He knows all about you—or as much as anyone knows about you. He's very suspicious of you, John. Very suspicious.''

''He thinks I'm a spy—or a smuggler? No, don't tell me. I'm *both!*'' Alastair guessed, barely able to keep a straight face. So much for the investigative arm of His Majesty's Preventive Service! He was pleased he had told Wiggins to keep the good Lieutenant in the dark as to his true identity. The man was obviously incompetent.

Elly leaned forward, as if to comfort him. ''Don't fly into the boughs, John. He just mentioned to me that he has investigated your background to find that you were never in the army. He finds that—and Hugo's presence—very disturbing. But he didn't actually make any accusations. He just kept referring to his infernal copybook.''

From the look on her face as she mentioned the copybook, Alastair deduced that Lieutenant Jason Fishbourne was not Elly's favorite Preventive Service officer. ''So he came to you with his doubts and suspicions? I have been out of touch. Is it customary to involve private citizens—especially female private citizens—in hunts for spies and smugglers?''

''You're upset, aren't you?''

Alastair decided that his beloved Elly was a master of understatement. Was he upset? Of course he was upset! How dare this Lieutenant involve her in this whole affair? ''I object to his tactics. He was using you, Elly, wasn't he?''

The bonnet strings were once more within her grasp and she began shredding one of them with her fingers. ''Not really, John. He visited Seashadow earlier to ask if I would report any strangers or unusual activities on the beaches. It was all quite congenial, really.'' Her head and her voice both lowered as she ended, ''Until today.''

''And what was different about today?''

She rose to examine the mantel clock, which kept her features away from his sight. ''He all but accused you of being a spy—or a smuggler. I think he was leaning toward your being a spy. And—and he wanted to know why I hadn't reported your presence at Seashadow. He, or his men, have been watching our every movement—and he has recorded it all in his little copybook, just like a schoolboy at his sums.''

Alastair rose to stand beside her, his hand lightly caressing her shoulder. ''I see. I believe I should like to meet this Lieutenant Fishbourne, just so that I might give him a good pop in his nose. And what did you tell him, Elly? What reason did you give for not reporting me like any loyal citizen should?''

''I told him we were—'' the rest was unintelligible.

"You told him what?" Alastair pressed, leaning closer, the better to hear her.

"Betrothed!" she all but shouted, turning about to face him. "I told him we were betrothed. And then I invited him to join us all for dinner tomorrow night at Seashadow because you were away somewhere today visiting your doctor for that nonexistent wound to your leg. But I didn't do it so that you could give him a good pop on the nose. I figured I could give you some time to get away before he could arrest you. There! Are you happy now?"

Happy? Alastair was ecstatic. She had lied for him. She had covered up for him, even while believing that there could be some truth to the Lieutenant's wild accusations. She loved him. Oh, yes she did, whether she admitted it or not. Alastair's smile was so wide, it threatened to crack his face in two.

"Will you help me pack my bags, dearest Elly? I should leave before the tide turns, don't you think, if I want to rendezvous with my froggie friends in Calais. You are free to accompany me if you wish, but I will understand if you refuse and want to cry off from our engagement."

Her complexion deepened to a becoming dusky pink for a moment before she drew herself up straight and declared with some heat, "Stop it! Don't you try to bamboozle me with your nonsense, John."

He grabbed at his chest, as if her words had stung him to the quick. "Me? I wouldn't be so brave. How am I trying to bamboozle you?"

She shook her head in exasperation. "You're no more a spy than Leslie is."

"Then I'm to be a smuggler?" he asked, not quite

liking the look in her eyes. She wasn't just watching him; she was examining him from head to foot, as if measuring him for a suit of clothes.

"No," she answered, shaking her head, "you're not a smuggler either. I don't know why I didn't see it sooner, but I know now *exactly* what—or should I say *who*—you are."

"Then what am I, Elly? And why are you protecting me from the good Lieutenant?"

"You're Alastair Lowell, Fourteenth Earl of Hythe—*that's* who you are, John—and I think I hate you very, very much!"

Her words had Alastair hunting blindly for the hard wooden settle before his knees gave out from beneath him. So much for struggling with himself all during a long, sleepless night, trying to decide how to break the news to her in the kindest way possible.

"I'm right, aren't I? Oh, of course I am—it's written all over your face. I can see your guilty expression straight through that horrid beard. Oh, John, how could you?"

How could he? How could she have guessed? "Wh—what gave me away?"

"Then it is true," she said fatally, looking down at him. "I had so hoped I was wrong." He watched as Elly sat down on the facing settle with a thump, her body folding in on itself like a bladder that has lost all its air. "I was packing away the Earl's clothing the other day. You're exactly the same size. You knew precisely where we keep the brandy. Mrs. Biggs wanted Big George to serve your favorite dish, and lied badly when I asked her to explain how she knew what it was. You were too arrogant to be a lowly soldier, as you claimed, and you have no calluses. So many little things," she told him quietly. "Oh, my poor, poor Leslie. Misfortune seems to dog his every footstep. Whatever will he do now?"

"He'll have to find himself a new studio, for one thing," Alastair was stung into saying, for he found he disliked intensely the fact that Elly had stolen his thunder—and all because of stuffed capon and calluses— "while I try to find another billiards table as good as the one he ruined."

Elly now glared up at him, her slanted brown eyes swimming with tears. "Your billiards table. Is that all you can think of, John—my lord?"

He was instantly contrite, for it was obvious that her whole world had just been shattered. Quickly sliding down from the settle to rest on his knees before her, Alastair reached out to take hold of Elly's elbows. "Not 'my lord,' dearest Elly, never 'my lord.' My name is Alastair."

He felt himself begin pushed backward as she hopped to her feet, putting as much space between the two of them as the small room allowed. "Alastair? Hardly, my lord—and I am not your *dearest* anything!" she exclaimed, flinging her hands wide. "Call yourself Judas, or Benedict, for you are the most two-faced, self-serving monster in all England! How dare you give Leslie false hope? How dare you come sneaking around here, checking up on your successor and telling all sorts of lies for your own amusement— in aid or your own twisted little game?"

Alastair's shoulders sagged for a moment as he considered her charges, then he straightened as he heard her call his actions a game. "Games, is it, Miss Dalrymple? And what sort of game is it to conk someone over the head and then dump him overboard to drown? Perhaps you can give me the name of this game, as I don't recognize it."

His words seemed to stop her from barreling out of the cottage, probably following hard on the heels of some dire warning concerning her wish never to see him again. "You—you didn't *fall* overboard?"

Alastair smiled. Yes, she was an intelligent puss. "No, Elly. I didn't fall overboard. Nor was I drunk— well, no more than two parts drunk anyway. I was pushed. If it hadn't been for Hugo, I would have drowned. As it was, it was two weeks until I came around, and nearly another two until I was fit to travel here."

"To find Leslie installed as the Earl," Elly finished for him, coming back to sit down once more. "But why didn't you announce yourself alive and reclaim your title immediately?"

"Would you?" Alastair asked, sitting down beside her and taking one of her cold hands in his. "Someone had just tried to kill me, Elly. I decided to hide away here, at Seashadow, until I could figure out who wanted me dead."

She pulled her hand away. "And so you settled on Leslie?"

Elly might have stumbled onto his true identity through the backdoor, but she was certainly heading in the right direction now, for a moment later she turned to him to screech: "No! Anyone could see that Leslie wouldn't hurt a fly. You thought *I* was the one who wanted you dead! Don't try to deny it. That's why you were so nice to me—you were trying to worm your way into Seashadow while you decided how to unmask me for the criminal you think I am. Oh, John, how could you?''

There was, Alastair had learned over the course of the years, a time for truth and a time for lies. This was a time for lies. ''How could you ever think such a thing, Elly—after all we have been to each other?'' he exclaimed with as much umbrage as he could muster. ''I came here to discover who wanted me dead, yes, but not because I thought you or Leslie was the culprit. Far from it. I hadn't even known of your existence. I came here looking for the spies or smugglers who wanted me out of the way so that they could use my beaches undisturbed. I'm hurt, Elly, hurt to the quick, that you could think such a thing of me.''

He turned away from her, silently praying that his half-truth would be acceptable. Besides, his mention of spies and smugglers hopefully might have jogged her memory about her own barely masked suspicions of him—not to mention her several disparaging statements about the late Earl made in his presence.

''You're working for the government?'' she asked weakly after a few moments.

He turned back to face her, his smile deliberately guileless. ''In a manner of speaking. I am working with Captain Geoffrey Wiggins, who is connected to the War Office.''

''I'm terribly confused.''

That makes two of us, Alastair thought silently, but he knew better than to share his confusion with Elly. Instead, he slid an arm around her shoulders, pulling her against him. ''It's very simple, my dear. I am here incognito, working to unmask the spy who has been

using Seashadow's beaches as his stopping-off point
on his way back and forth from London to France.
Once everyone in the chain has been captured—including the bounder who tried to do me in—I shall
announce my lucky escape from a watery grave and
resume my customary hey-go-mad place in Society,
with no one being the wiser that I have, in reality,
been a contributing member to the war effort.''

"Leaving Leslie to crawl back to obscurity and his
two hundred pounds a year,'' Elly ended in a very
small voice, leaning her head against his shoulder.
"How I shall detest eating turnips again.''

"Not necessarily, my pet,'' Alastair told her, knowing he was dragging the thing out but feeling he was
getting a little of his own back for having to listen to
her tear his reputation to shreds more than once.
"There is still the small matter of our betrothal. I had,
of course, entertained hopes—but as I had yet to speak
to your brother, I am all ears to hear the details of this
recent engagement between us.''

"Oh, aren't you just,'' Elly snapped, pulling her
head away. "I certainly wasn't serious about the thing,
you know. You had pretended an interest in me in
order to get into Seashadow, and I had simply taken
a page from your book in using the supposed betrothal
to put Lieutenant Fishbourne off the scent. We are not
truly engaged.''

He pulled her head back against his shoulder once
more. "And you are that set against it, then, dearest
Elly? Think about it. Leslie would have his studio—a
separate studio on each of my holdings—and you
would never have to stare down another horrid turnip.
I should think you'd jump at the chance.''

Elly pushed his arm away and stood, glaring down at him. "You're laughing at me. I suppose I deserve it, for saying all those nasty things about you—and for thinking you might be a spy, for I did think that for a while, and if you think I believe for one moment that you hadn't harbored the thought that I was the one who tried to drown you, you're sadly mistaken—but I don't think I should have to stay here and be insulted. Good day to you, my lord Hythe! Leslie and I will be gone in the morning."

"And where will you go?" Alastair asked, also rising.

That question stopped her, as he had been sure it would. "Oh, do be quiet!" she ordered, bending to pick up her bonnet. "I have to think. I can't have an answer for everything, you know."

"Seashadow is a great barn of a place—although it is the smallest of my estates. You could stay there for a while without too much danger of the two of us stumbling over each other. I am going to take up residence now, you understand—out of consideration for Hugo's poor head, that keeps making its acquaintance with the lintels of this charming cottage, and in order to be closer to Big George's kitchen. Then there is the matter of the person who is trying to kill Leslie."

He watched, entranced, as Elly's eyes got very wide. "Someone—someone is trying to kill Leslie? I don't believe it!"

He shrugged. "Why not? Someone tried to kill me when I was the Earl of Hythe, in order to have access to Seashadow's beaches. Why wouldn't he try to kill the new Earl of Hythe, who cropped up unexpectedly when no heir was expected to surface? Leslie has been shot at, you know, and more than once. I was witness to the latest attempt yesterday afternoon just minutes after you left us—although Leslie will be angry that I've told you about it, fearing that you won't allow him outside any more. That's why Hugo is at Seashadow, to guard Leslie. We may be dealing with an inept murderer, but his luck is bound to change sooner or later.''

Elly spread her hands. ''But now that *you're* the Earl again, no one will be after Leslie,'' she deduced, to Alastair's mind, entirely too clearly. ''My brother will be safe the moment you make your announcement.''

''And in danger the moment I'm really dead,'' Alastair pointed out, trying his best not to succumb to the urge to strangle her for so blithely whistling *his* safety down the wind. ''Besides, what makes you think I'm going to make any announcements? I'm still working with Wiggins. My identity has to remain a secret until all the spies are captured. I will merely be residing at Seashadow, as Leslie's guest.''

''You-you'd deliberately put Leslie in danger?'' Elly questioned, clearly incensed. ''How could you be so cruel?''

''Leslie is in no danger, now that Hugo is taking care of him. As a matter of fact, I do believe Hugo has already saved your brother once—that day on the cliff—although I'm convinced we'll never understand exactly what happened. But since late yesterday, when I was witness to an attempt on Leslie's life, Seashadow has been patrolled by my mea, with Harry leading them, and Leslie hasn't been out of Hugo's sight. The only thing I don't understand is how Harry let you slip past him to come to the cottage.''

CHAPTER SEVEN

"I ALREADY TOLD YOU, John," Elly answered absently, for her head was still reeling from all that had happened to her today. "The Biggses are all sick in their beds—all except Rosie, who has gotten better and Lily, who is less than useless, sick or well. Are you really going to move in at Seashadow and hide behind Leslie while attempting to uncover the person or persons who tried to kill you?"

She watched as John—Alastair—winced. "When you say it like that, it doesn't sound very noble, does it, Elly? But, yes, that is exactly what I propose to do. Our murderer will think twice about striking again if he learns that his first attempt on me failed. He'd go straight to ground, not to resurface for months to make another attempt. I want this over and done with as quickly as possible, for I want to get back to London and my life there."

"Your life in London! Is that all it means to you— that you have to be away from the gaming tables and your...your painted ladies? It's almost as if you're doing all of this as a sort of lark. I take back every kind word I ever said about you!" Elly pronounced feelingly.

Alastair only shrugged at this insult, making her more angry than before. "No matter. There can't have

been more than two or three of them at best anyway—
kind words, that is. If you only knew how trying it
was for me to sit back and do nothing while, time after
time, you threw my past in my teeth. As a matter of
fact, you just did it again, didn't you? Now, Elly, if
you are through surprising me with your brilliant de-
ductive powers, and done accusing me of hiding behind your brother's skinny legs, perhaps we can have
a serious discussion.''

Now, why did she know they weren't going to talk
about their supposed engagement, the one he persisted
in pretending to be real? Was it because he had just
told her he wanted to get back to his life in London?
Of course it was. She didn't have to be hit over the
head with a red brick to know that he had all but
forgotten her already. ''What do you wish to discuss,
John?'' she asked, settling herself once more on one
of the wooden settles.

''Good. That's very good, Elly. Continue to address
me as John. It would be too easy to trip up with Fishbourne or anyone else who may be about if you tried
to call me Alastair in private and John when we are
in public.''

Elly nodded and nervously bit her lower lip. She
hadn't realized that she had called him John. But there
was no John, was there? The John who had walked
the beach with her was gone, to be replaced by a mon-
ied, titled peer who wanted nothing to do with a silly,
suspicious spinster who thought that taking down her
hair could change her into a lovable, desirable woman.
She was being silly—feeling as if she would like to
have a quiet period of mourning to mark his passing

before having to deal with the overpowering Alastair Lowell, Earl of Hythe.

Good lord! Alastair was the Earl of Hythe! How long would it take before she could say those words, even think those words, without a stab of real physical pain cutting into her heart?

Oh, her poor, poor Leslie! It wasn't just his life that was in danger. She raised a hand to her head, Alastair's mention of her brother bringing back her other worries. How was she ever going to tell Leslie he was no longer the Earl?

And wherever would they go? They had given up their small leased cottage in Linton, and they had precious little funds left to secure another one. How difficult it would be to leave Seashadow and the beach they had both grown to love. How difficult it would be to leave John—Alastair—a man she really didn't know, yet a man who already meant more to her than the very air she breathed.

"Elly?"

She shook her head, purposely banishing all depressing thoughts of a future without Alastair from her mind. "When do you wish to take up your chambers at Seashadow?" she asked, praying her voice was steady. "I just aired them the other day—as Leslie didn't wish to occupy them—and your clothes have all been packed away in the attics. I suppose I could have them ready for you by this evening, if I can get Lily to help."

She looked up at him as another thought struck her. "Lily! She knew, didn't she? No, don't answer. Of course she knew—and she used the opportunity to flirt outrageously with you that night you first came to dinner. The little minx!''

Alastair smiled, and she suddenly longed to rip out his beard, one blonde hair at a time. "So that still rankles, does it? Yes, I had forgotten that Lily and I will now be under the same roof. You know, she has *blossomed* quite nicely since my last visit to Seashadow," he commented, stroking that same beard.

"You wouldn't!"

"I wouldn't what, dearest Elly?" he responded, continuing to smile a moment more before sobering. "Of course I wouldn't. Is your opinion of Alastair Lowell still that low? I am an engaged man, remember? You told me so yourself. You told Lieutenant Fishbourne. Have you sent notices to the papers as yet, or are you going to leave at least that much up to me?"

It had been a very trying twenty-four hours for Elly. She had been dreadfully ill for a large part of it, for one thing. Then there had been that distressing interview with the so pompous, so suspicious Lieutenant Fishbourne. And, as if that were not enough, she had learned that her worst imaginings about John Bates were founded in fact—and that she and Leslie were about to be dispossessed.

Having Alastair joke about her lies to Lieutenant Fishbourne, having him tease her with wild hopes that could never be fulfilled, was simply more than she could endure. Elly jumped up from the settle, brought back her right hand, and swung from her heels, landing a loud, stinging openhanded slap directly to Alastair's left cheek.

A moment later Elly was wrapped in Alastair's arms

and his mouth was against hers, his kiss warm and deep and seemingly full of passion. She should struggle, she knew she should, but all the fight had suddenly gone out of her, to be replaced with her overriding need of this infuriating man.

She allowed her hands to creep up Alastair's broad chest, to entwine themselves behind his neck, just as his hands moved upward to the pins in her hair, removing them one by one so that her curls tumbled down past her shoulders.

She felt free, she felt reborn, she felt as if she were the most beautiful, desirable woman in all England. Opening her eyes to peek at him, she could see that Alastair's eyes were squeezed shut, as if he was intent on what he was doing, intent on kissing her until she either fainted or went mad.

Her toes were curling inside her jean half boots before he finally broke the kiss, but it was only to push her head against his chest, his fingers still deeply tangled in her hair, his arms still holding her a willing captive.

She touched her fingertips to her bruised mouth. ''I detest that beard,'' she mumbled against his waistcoat, saying the first thing that came into her mind. ''It scratches.''

She sensed more than heard the rumble of his laughter. ''It itches, too—and it will be the first thing to go once I am free to announce that I am still alive. As a matter of fact, my pet, if you wish to make a list—I understand from Leslie that you are partial to them— I shall be doing three things once the people who want me dead are safely locked up. One, I shall remove to London to reclaim my estates—for they do not run themselves, you know. Two, I shall shave. And three, I shall announce our engagement in all the papers, so that I don't have to be slapped anymore. You are quite strong for a little thing, you know, my pet. In fact, now that I think of it, perhaps numbers two and three should be reversed—just for the sake of my personal safety.''

Elly pulled slightly away from him—his arms were not about to let her move much farther—and asked, "You are serious, Alastair? You really do want to marry me? I mean, this isn't another rig you are running? Another game you are playing? You really, *really* want to marry me? Why?"

She watched as his brow furrowed. "Dear Elly, always so full of doubts. Do you know what, Elly? I really don't know why. I've never wanted to shackle myself to anyone before. I only know that you are the most inquisitive—I'm sure I should dare to say nosy—female I have ever met; a woman who is as beautiful as she is intelligent, and as loyal and courageous as she is foolhardy."

"I am not foolhardy," Elly replied, stung by his last word even as she gloried in most of what had come before it.

He leaned down to place a kiss on the tip of her nose. "You flirted with me in the most outrageous way, all to keep my interest while you delved into my life to see if I was a smuggler, or a Bonapartist spy. If that isn't foolhardy enough for you, my dear, allow me to point out that you are now standing alone with me in this cottage—our bodies pressed tightly together, knee to neck—with no chaperone about and your beloved thinking delightful thoughts that have no business being in his head until after our marriage.''

''Wretch,'' Elly grumbled, removing herself from his embrace, her head bowed so that he could not see the hot color that had invaded her cheeks. She reached behind her for her bonnet. ''You are lucky that I am so very old, or you wouldn't have me swooning, you know. I had better leave now, I imagine?''

''That would be best, I suppose, although I don't like it—and you are not old. You are just right.'' Alastair took the bonnet from her hand and placed it on her head, arranging her long blonde hair around her shoulders before neatly tying the ribbons beneath her chin. ''I'll walk with you to Seashadow and send Hugo back for our things and to close up the cottage. You'll see, Elly. We'll all be as merry as grigs.''

Big George had recovered sufficiently to prepare a simple meal that evening, after which Leslie, Hugo, Alastair, and Elly repaired to the drawing room, where they now sat, Leslie and Hugo at the far side of the room playing spillikins, Alastair and Elly sitting side by side on the settee, holding hands.

''Tell me all about Hugo, dearest,'' Elly asked, smiling as the giant let out a roar at winning yet another game.

'' 'Dearest,' '' Alastair repeated, squeezing her hand. ''I think I like that.''

Elly blushed. It occurred to her that she had blushed more since meeting Alastair than she had ever done before in her life. ''It seemed a good compromise,'' she told him. ''This way I cannot possibly call you

Alastair when I should be addressing you as John. You don't mind, do you?''

She watched as he lifted her hand to his mouth and placed a gentle kiss in her palm. "I like it excessively, to tell you the truth. But, as it can lead nowhere for some time, I will do my best to take it in my stride and not allow my emotions to overwhelm me. Now, tell me, what else do you want to learn about my good friend Hugo? I've already told you that he rescued me from a watery grave.''

Elly closed her fingers around the palm that still burned from the imprint of Alastair's kiss. "What?'' she asked, her train of thought hopelessly jumbled by his romantic action. "Oh, yes, Hugo. I was just wondering how he came to have his tongue cut out. You had told me it was cut out, hadn't you?''

Alastair reached into his pocket and withdrew the letter Hugo had placed in his keeping. "This is all I know,'' he said, handing her the paper. "I recopied the note he carried—his mother had dictated it to explain his condition—as this one has seen better days. I'd like to keep it with Seashadow's other important documents as it is very valuable to Hugo.''

When she had finished reading the letter, there were tears in Elly's eyes. She carefully folded the paper and handed it back to Alastair before searching in the pocket of her gown for her handkerchief. "That's terribly sad, isn't it? And yet Hugo is so gentle, so loving.''

Alastair nodded. "And he's not a jaw-me-dead either. All I have to do is close my eyes, and I can't hear him.''

"For shame! I would be angry with you if I could

believe you aren't merely saying that to upset me. You and Hugo are good friends. However, Leslie is absolutely dotty about him.''

"Leslie, my love, is dotty about everything. Which is why I am happy you've agreed with me that we should keep my identity a secret from him for a while longer. It will be enough for him to handle the fact that he is no longer the Earl. But you have to own it, knowing that someone is trying to erase him from the face of the earth may be too much for him to take in.''

"Well, that's that," Leslie said loudly, rising from his chair to come across the room to where Elly and Alastair sat, so that Elly could not remind Alastair that she had never really agreed with his plan to keep her brother in the dark as to the facts. "He won every game. Devilish acute, Hugo is, John, as I just taught him the game. I say, Elly, you're looking pinched. Stomach still upset?''

"Leslie," she said tightly, as Alastair was squeezing her hand in warning, "you will remember to take Hugo with you everywhere you go, won't you?''

Her brother smiled down at her, shaking his head. "Of course I shall, Elly. Haven't you told me a dozen times tonight that Hugo is feeling lost in this big house and I should be responsible for him?''

"Maybe she'd like to embroider it on a pair of garters for you," Alastair teased, earning himself a searching look from his beloved.

"No," Leslie replied, obviously believing Alastair to be serious. "Can't knit—stands to reason she can't embroider either. I say, John, would it be all right if Hugo and I went to my studio? I promised him I would show him my collection of grasshoppers.''

Alastair agreed immediately, causing Elly to wonder if perhaps, at last, she could feel free to ask him some questions that had been burning in her head the whole time she had been dressing for dinner.

"I'd like to hear more about Captain Wiggins, if you please," she informed him once Leslie and Hugo were gone. "I don't quite understand his part in any of this."

For the next quarter hour Elly listened as Alastair brought her up-to-date on everything that had happened from the first time Captain Wiggins had been ushered into the drawing room of Alastair's London town house to the moment the spy and smugglers had landed on the beach at Seashadow.

"You saw the smugglers—and the spy?" she broke in as he seemed to digress from his story for a moment, to concentrate on the perils of half burying one's body in insect-infested sand, a tale that, to her mind, had precious little to do with capturing spies and smugglers. "And you did nothing? They're still out there, running about somewhere?"

"I wouldn't say that we did nothing, pet," Alastair answered with maddening calm. "We counted them. Geoffrey is very big on counting—but that really doesn't matter anymore. According to my latest communication from the good Captain, who has been so kind as to keep me fully informed, the spy's connection in London has been neutralized—I believe that is the word Geoffrey used—so all that remains is to pretend to capture the spy himself when he attempts a return to France. According to the phases of the moon, that should be any time now."

"*Pretend* to capture the spy. *Count* the smugglers."

Elly thought she was going to scream. "Is this the way we are winning the war, Alastair? You're not making any sense! If you don't want to tell me the truth—if you think my female brain is not capable of absorbing the ins and outs of such intrigues—please have the goodness not to lie so outrageously. Pretend to capture the spy, indeed. You're trying to gull me."

"Please, pet, don't descend to cant, especially just as I am determined to mature myself. Besides, I am not *gulling* you. The spy has been given a fistful of erroneous information bound to have a good portion of Napoleon's forces chasing their own tails while Wellington advances toward France unscathed. It is a good plan, bordering on brilliant, actually, which is why I am so surprised Wiggins thought of it."

Elly was quiet for a while, trying to absorb all the information she had received, mentally separating the wheat from the chaff. After a lifetime of dealing with Leslie, sorting out the pertinent information contained within Alastair's tale was not that difficult.

"There's going to be some action on the beach at Seashadow very shortly, isn't there, John?"

"Dearest. You were going to call me dearest," Alastair reminded her, giving her a kiss on the cheek. "I don't know why women have such a reputation for being devious, when you cannot even seem to keep my name straight, my love."

She pushed him away. "Don't distract me," she ordered, refusing to melt beneath his careless charm. "You said Captain Wiggins is going to pretend to capture the spy. Why would he want to do that, if you want the spy to take incorrect information to France? And I thought you wanted to capture the spy—who is most probably behind the attempts on your life, and Leslie's. Maybe you're right, and this is all beyond a mere female's mind.''

Alastair raised her hand to his lips once more. ''Don't frown, pet, and don't think unkindly of yourself. It really is quite convoluted. Now look—the traitor in the War Office has been captured, but that doesn't mean our spy knows this. So he will also not think his identity or whereabouts is known to us—allowing him to feel free to leave England the way he came to it, via the beach at Seashadow. That's why they chose my section of the coastline, you know. It is a natural harbor, and away from any real population.''

Elly nodded. ''All right. I understand you so far. Go on.''

''As we know who the spy is, we can follow his every movement, and be on hand as he waits on the beach for the smugglers he has hired to transport him to row in to the shore.''

''So that you can pretend to capture him? No, it still doesn't make sense.''

''It does once you know that the spy that will be waiting for the smugglers on the beach will not be the real spy,'' Alastair said, his expression smug as he gave her this last piece of information.

Elly sat back and gnawed on the right side of her thumb as she considered everything Alastair had said. ''If Wiggins captures the *real* spy at the last minute, and replaces him with his *own* spy—making sure the man has to run full tilt to the boat to evade certain capture, so that the smugglers are too fully occupied outrunning the soldiers to check his identity too closely—he can be safely out at sea under cover of darkness and delivered to France without anyone on the boat being the wiser! It's brilliant!''

Alastair slipped an arm across her shoulders. "Yes, I thought so myself."

Suddenly Elly sat front, Alastair's arm falling away from her shoulders. "No—it's not brilliant. How will our spy know what to do when he gets to France? He'll be exposed and captured—and *executed!*''

"No, he won't. Wiggins has been a very busy little bee and learned exactly what the spy will have to do once the boat docks. All he has to do is enter a certain small tavern on the waterfront—The Cold Heart is, I believe, the English translation—sit at the second table from the door, the hood of his black cloak pulled down low over his eyes, and wait for a barmaid named Yvette.

"She will place a tray on the table, he will place the information on the tray, and that will be that. Oh, yes, I believe our spy will also pick up some information from Yvette—which can only be considered a lovely bonus, Wiggins says.

"The spy will then be free to return to England immediately, his smuggler cohorts having waited for him. Within twenty-four hours—once the smugglers are once more nearing our shores, a Preventive cutter will pick them up, rescuing our spy before the light of day can give him away."

She leaned back again, snuggling into his embrace. "You were right. It is brilliant. How I envy the man who is going to be able to engage in such an invigorating scheme."

"Yes," Alastair said, pulling her close. "I imagine

it will be something a man would wish to tell his children about someday. We are going to have children, aren't we? I mean, I think Leslie is a wonderful fellow, but I couldn't rest easy in my grave, knowing he was systematically destroying every last one of my estates with his paint pots and projects.''

Elly pulled slightly away from him, to stare up into his face. ''You're not—I mean, you wouldn't consider—you couldn't possibly be—'' she began nervously.

''I couldn't possibly be what, my darling Elly?'' Alastair asked, playing with a lock of blonde hair that had fallen forward onto her forehead. ''Have I told you yet that I love you, pet? I do, you know, most desperately.''

He looked so young, so wonderfully attractive, so gently loving. He wouldn't get himself involved with such a dangerous mission. She was being silly, overreacting because she had already lost Robert to this miserable war that seemed to be dragging on forever. Besides, this Wiggins fellow sounded capable. He wouldn't leave such an important mission in the hands of an amateur.

Yet it wouldn't hurt to ask him, would it? After all, they were betrothed. He wouldn't lie to her now—maybe once, but not now.

''Dearest,'' she began, careful to use the term of endearment they had agreed upon, ''you would never do anything dangerous, would you? I mean, Captain Wiggins seems to have it all planned out so nicely and all. Once the spy and the smugglers are captured, you and Leslie will be safe and we can get on with our lives. You don't feel any need to be *personally* involved beyond what you have done, do you?''

"Me?" she heard him answer, his tone comfortingly incredulous. "Don't be ridiculous, my pet. My mission is to keep my identity hidden and Leslie out of the line of fire until Geoffrey is done playing at his little games. After all you have learned about me and my self-serving, devil-may-care, ramshackle existence—which ended the moment I met you, my darling—can you really believe I would ever consider endangering myself on purpose?"

"No, I suppose not," Elly agreed softly, feeling his fingers reaching beneath her chin to raise her face for his kiss.

"Whoops! I seem to have come in at an inopportune moment, haven't I, John, old man. Sorry about that. I didn't know the two of you were so chummy. I'll knock next time."

Elly looked across the room to see her brother about to leave. "What did you want, Leslie?" she asked, amused by her brother's total lack of outrage at seeing his sister being ruthlessly kissed by a man who was a guest in their house.

Leslie turned back to face them. "It's really not all that important, I guess, Elly—and I am in a bit of a rush. Just carry on," he suggested with a wave of his hand.

"Your sister and I are to be married, my lord, if it suits you," Alastair announced, rising. "I know this is a terrible breach of good form, and that I should have asked your permission first, but as Elly is of age and all—"

Leslie flapped his arms wildly, as if impatient with

Alastair's explanation and in a hurry to be gone. "Yes, yes, whatever you want. I have more pressing matters myself. Wait a minute. Elly—since you're not busy now—I have to ask. You did say I was to take Hugo with me everywhere, didn't you?"

"Yes, my dearest," Elly agreed, marveling at the ease with which Leslie took the news of her betrothal. "I did say that."

The arms flapped again, as Leslie began to do a little dance. "Well, Elly, the thing of it is—I have to visit the—that is—do I have to take him *everywhere* with me?"

Alastair fell back onto the settee, roaring with laughter, earning himself a poke in the ribs from his beloved.

"No, Leslie," Elly choked out, trying not to succumb to a similar fit of hysterics, "you do not have to take Hugo with you when you go *there*."

Elly and Alastair hung together, laughing until there sides ached, long after Leslie had sprinted out of the drawing room, all thoughts of spies and smugglers forgotten.

ALASTAIR STOOD contemplating his reflection in the large mirror in his chamber, wondering if it would be possible for him to remove his beard without the help of his valet, Albert, who was still in London. "Probably eating his head off in my town house, when he isn't cavorting on my bed with the upstairs maid, that is," he told himself, his eyes narrowing at the thought.

Having spent a restful night in the familiarity of his own bed at Seashadow—probably the most restful night he'd had since his dunk in the Channel—Alastair was more anxious than ever to have the business of his attempted murder behind him so that he could get on with his life.

Marriage. Who would believe it? It was amazing. A few months ago, prior to his dunking, the mere mention of the word would have put him in full flight— to Scotland or some other remote, primitive place where men hunted and fished and did other manly things that did not require the company of women. As a matter of fact, the only thing they did require was the total *absence* of the fairer sex.

And she was fair, his Elly. *His Elly.* Even spoken silently, within the confines of his own mind, the words sounded incredibly sweet. What had he ever done to deserve her? After hearing Elly tell him about Robert Talmadge, her onetime fiancé who had given up his life for his country, he was even more sure of the course he was about to take, more certain that he should have to *earn* her love, and not be satisfied to have simply stumbled onto it, the same way one would stumble onto a four-leaf clover.

Picking up his tan hacking jacket—the one he'd had made for him last year at Weston's—Alastair sauntered out of his bedchamber in search of his betrothed, hopeful of spending a restful interlude with her on the beach while he waited for his summons from Wiggins.

"Hallo, *John*," Lily Biggs cooed, coming out of one of the bedchambers to step directly in front of him as he neared the staircase. "Ain't yer a treat, all dressed up in the old Earl's duds?"

"Thank you, Lily," Alastair said, moving to his right, to pass by her. He wasn't in the mood for one of Lily's childish attempts at seduction.

She stepped in front of him again. "I wonder what that handsome Lieutenant would think ter learn wot yer about, *Johnny?* Mighty interested in yer, the Lieutenant is or so I heard him say ter that Dalrymple woman yesterday."

"Is that right? That Dalrymple woman is your mistress, if you'll remember." Alastair stood quietly as Lily reached out to take hold of his lapels, using them to pull herself closer, so that their bodies were pressed together. "You're not too old to spank, Lily," he warned quietly.

"Oooh—a spankin'," she trilled, grinding her hips against him. "I think I might jist like that, *Johnny.*"

Alastair reached up to disengage Lily's hands from his hacking jacket. "You have quite a future on your back, Lily, if Billie or Big George don't kill you first. Now, let me get this straight, just so that we don't misunderstand each other. You're threatening me, aren't you, little one? What exactly do you want?"

Lily smiled, her pointed pink tongue coming out to moisten her upper lip. "Wot does I wants, Johnny? I should think yer'd know. I heared about yer when yer were younger, when yer used to come here with all yer fine friends. I jist wants a little fun—a little tickle."

Alastair smiled as he looked down at the girls full half-exposed bosom, disbelieving that the gods would do this to him now, just when he had decided to become a sober, responsible citizen. If Lily were not a Biggs, if he had never heard of a small firebrand named Elinor Dalrymple, he would most probably already be pulling the girl back into his bedchamber.

"You don't have the term quite right, Lily," he

heard himself say. "It's not just tickle. It's 'slap and tickle,' if memory serves."

The tongue appeared once more, as well as a provocative dimple in her left cheek. "I guess yer'll just have ter show me, Johnny," she purred, her hands dropping to his waist.

"I guess I just will," Alastair answered shortly, grabbing her by both hands and all but dragging her down the hall to his bedchamber. Once inside the room, he closed and locked the door before sitting down on the side of the wide bed. "Come here to me, Lily," he commanded softly.

Smiling, her hips exaggeratedly swinging from side to side, Lily approached the bed and sat down on Alastair's lap. "Ooooh, this is nice, ain't it?" she remarked, collapsing against him.

A moment later Lily was lying facedown across Alastair's lap and he was delivering the first of a half dozen stinging slaps to her rounded bottom.

When he was done, he allowed her to slide to the floor, where she sat looking up at him, her eyes filled with tears—and all the hate a sixteen-year-old girl could muster. "Wot did yer go and do that fer?" she screamed at him.

"I decided it was time to teach you a lesson, Lily," he said as kindly as he could. "Never threaten a man, my dear little girl. We're bigger than you are. Now, we'll keep this between us, as I wouldn't want your mother and father upset."

Not waiting to hear whether or not she agreed with him, Alastair left the room once again, more eager than before to find Elly. Thank God he had her love, for if he had survived his spill into the ocean only to return to a life filled with Lilys—a life he had formerly exulted in—he would rather have drowned!

He passed Billie Biggs—who was standing at the open front doors directing Iris as the child diligently scrubbed the steps with a brown brush—and walked out into the sunlight to see Leslie Dalrymple skipping across the gravel drive.

Alastair frowned. Where was Hugo? He shook his head and started forward. Obviously Leslie had slipped his leash, and now it was up to him to fetch the runaway home again. "Leslie!" he called out loudly, and the young man whirled about—a wide, childish smile on his vacantly handsome face—just as a shot rang out. A moment later, clutching his left shoulder, Leslie crumpled to the ground.

CHAPTER EIGHT

"AH, THERE YOU ARE, my dear. I thought I might find you in here. I suppose you want to tear out my guts and feed them to the crows—and as it would be mean of me to hide and rob you of your pleasure, I came seeking you. Unless, that is, you've forgiven me, and you didn't mean what you said earlier when we met outside. I didn't know you knew such terrible words, truly I didn't. I was quite shocked, I tell you."

Elly's hands stopped in the midst of rearranging the bed pillows. "*You!* What do you want in here? Get out! Haven't you already done enough damage? Or are you lurking around here to inspect the results of your indefensible tactics?" She turned back to the bed after dismissing Alastair, intent on arranging Leslie's pillows behind his head.

How dare he come in here so blithely—and how dare he mention her temporary loss of control as Hugo had gently lifted a moaning Leslie to carry him inside? Blinking back traitorous tears she didn't want Alastair to see, Elly could still feel his presence in the chamber as she fluffed the feather pillows to within an inch of their lives, earning herself a whining rebuke from her brother.

"I say, Elly, leave off, do," Leslie told her. "I want to lie back now. You picked a plaguey queer time to be arguing, Elly. I'm not well, you know. And why are you angry with John anyway? He didn't shoot me, did he? No, of course he didn't. He wouldn't.''

''No, Leslie, I didn't. I wouldn't. It must have been those pesky poachers again. Poachers can be the very devil, can't they, as they have such poor aim. And yes, Elly, leave off, do,'' Alastair repeated from the foot of the bed. ''Perhaps I was wrong and you don't have designs on my internal organs, dear heart. I can live with that. But if you are upset over Leslie's accident and want to punch something, I'll volunteer myself for the job.''

Elly could hear the amusement in his voice—and the implied warning. He still didn't want her to say anything to Leslie. Although she felt he had been wrong to hide the danger from her brother, she agreed that it would serve no purpose to enlighten him now, after the fact.

But that didn't mean she had to be nice to Alastair. How dare he volunteer himself as a target for her anger, just as if she had gone stark, staring mad and he was the voice of reason? Of course she was angry with him—and he deserved every bit of it!

''And so you should, *John!*'' she exclaimed hotly, helping her brother to lie back, as his bandaged shoulder was making it difficult for him to manage the maneuver on his own. ''And stop acting the willing martyr, for I am unimpressed. How can you joke at a time like this, with Leslie lying here, at death's door.''

''Well, in matter of fact, Elly, I'm not exactly at death's door,'' Leslie corrected, looking up at his sister, who found herself momentarily wishing the bandage had been around his mouth.

"That's it, Leslie," Alastair exclaimed. "Pluck to the backbone. It would take more than one bullet to dampen your spirits!"

"Doctor Wallingsworth said it couldn't have been a nicer wound, what with the ball passing straight on through my arm the way it did without hitting anything even remotely important. There must actually be unimportant parts inside us, I suppose, although I can't imagine what they could be, for why else would we have them—if they weren't important for something? I would think the Almighty planned it better than that. Anyway, I should be up and about in a day or two, Doctor Wallingsworth said, and with this lovely sling and everything."

"Yes, Elly, he even has a lovely sling," Alastair agreed as she glared at him, not knowing whether it was anger or fear that had kept her temper simmering just below the boiling point ever since she had been summoned outside to see Leslie lying propped against Hugo's massive arms, a slowly spreading red stain on his shirt sleeve.

Simmering, except for that single, lamentable lapse during which she had employed a few words learned at her father's knee when that man had been fairly deep in his cups; she looked toward the object of her anger. "Oh, shut up," she said succinctly.

He seemed to be oblivious to her mood. "And it's his *left* arm into the bargain, so that his painting and whatever else it is that he does—and you do it all *very* well, dear Leslie—can go on uninterrupted. Wasn't that lucky?"

"Eh?" Leslie looked down at the sling, then at his right arm, and smiled. "By Jove, so it is, Elly. How about that! You are quite right, John. Thank you for pointing that out. I'm so very glad you have moved in with us until your roof can be patched. I may not have noticed my good fortune so quickly, if left to my own devices. I was indeed very lucky.''

''You're very welcome.''

Elly knew what Alastair was about, knew that he was trying to keep the situation light so as not to worry Leslie, but she just couldn't take it anymore. Her brother was much too gullible for words, and Alastair had no more sense than a newborn babe.

''Lucky?'' she exploded. ''*Lucky!* I don't know if the two of you are crazy and I'm sane—or if I am the one who should be carted away in her own straight-waistcoat. How can you call being shot lucky? Oh, I can see that I have to get away form the both of you for a while! Leslie, lie still.''

She brushed past Alastair and out of the room, only to turn on him as he followed her into the hall. ''Alastair, you *promised* me!'' she hissed, looking up at him, daring him to contradict her.

''Quietly, pet, so Leslie doesn't hear. There's no need to set him off again, is there? Elly, I know you're probably feeling mad as a baited bear, but—'' Alastair began.

She cut him off, not interested in what he might have to say in his own defense. She had things to do, and he was dreadfully in the way. ''You promised me Leslie would be all right. Hugo would take care of him, you said. It would all be over very soon, you said. There was no real danger, you said, as long as we did what *you said*. Well, you were *wrong*, Alastair—terribly wrong—and I don't think I shall ever be able to forgive you!''

"Well, I certainly hope someone forgives me,'' Alastair remarked, taking Elly's elbow against her will and leading her off down the hallway. "Am I heading you in the right direction, my dear? good!—for I am terribly depressed. I am also a victim, if you'll remember, and yet now I find myself cast in the role of villain. Hugo is completely out of charity with me—and if you have never been screamed at for a quarter hour by a very large someone who knows what *he* is saying, while *you* are totally in the dark, let me advise you not to actively encourage such an encounter—and Billie Biggs has gone so far as to threaten to have Big George take a birch rod to me. I think perhaps she has been in charge here too long, and considers me to be no better than the worst of her children.''

Elly did not pull her arm away, as Alastair's touch was comforting after her hours of fear for Leslie, and because she still loved this infuriating man very much—but that did not mean she was going to forgive him too easily.

"The fact that Leslie was shot at all *is* your responsibility, Alastair, as you were the one who insisted he not be told he was in danger. I knew I should have told him—which is probably why I am so angry. However did I let you talk me into not telling him? Leslie would never have slipped away from Hugo to walk outside looking for a thistle if you had told him not to do so. Leslie is very obedient—when he remembers what he is to be obedient about. But that is nothing to the point. He was never even warned.''

"Leslie was looking for a thistle?''

"He thought it would be above everything wonderful if he could use one as a sort of paint brush—but that's not important."

"Why do I know that you are now going to tell me precisely what *is* important?"

"You're absolutely right—for once. What's important is that you told me you had everything under control when in fact you didn't—you don't. Hugo couldn't have been more than three paces behind Leslie, and he couldn't save him. You've been treating this entire thing as some sort of entertaining intrigue, when in fact it is deadly serious. You may not have any great sense of self-preservation, but it wasn't enough that someone tried to kill you, was it? Oh, no. You couldn't rest until you had placed Leslie in danger as well. I cannot wait any longer to do what I have to do. I'm going to send a note round to Lieutenant Fishbourne immediately."

"Lieutenant Fishbourne? Tonight's dinner guest? How curious. This is, I suppose, the same pompous, full-of-himself fellow—and you told me this just last night, as I recall—who could bore paint into flaking off a wall?"

Prudently holding up her skirts as the two of them descended the staircase into the foyer, Elly nodded, noting that Alastair's memory was much like Leslie's—a steel trap when it came to remembering every verbal misstep *she* ever made.

"I did," she admitted crossly. "I never said I particularly *liked* the gentleman, Alastair. I just think it is time we called him in on this. You've already told me that your Captain Geoffrey Wiggins had been wanting to inform the Lieutenant all along, only you have refused to allow him to do so.''

Alastair guided her into the drawing room, where Mrs. Biggs had already placed the tea tray and a silver plate piled high with pastries. She knew she wouldn't be able to eat a single bite.

''And for good reason,'' he told her. ''Your so estimable Lieutenant has had ample time to capture the spy and has not done so. Why do you think Geoffrey came to me in the first place—because he was impressed with my winning smile?''

Elly bit her lip as she looked at Alastair. He was a wonderful man, really he was. He was loving, caring, full of good humor, and handsome into the bargain— and she still found it hard to believe that he really loved her. But he was also a Lowell. Her mother had been a Lowell. Leslie was also a Lowell. And Lowells were not known for their overwhelming sense of responsibility—or their keen understanding of basic common sense. Mostly they were just lovable.

She herself, Elly had long ago decided, must be a throwback to some commonsense paternal relative or, if not that, an exception to the Lowell rule. Each generation seemed to produce at least one responsible Lowell—or in this case, Dalrymple—whose sole purpose on this earth was to ride herd on the rest of the Lowells, protecting them from their own follies. She had fallen in love with Alastair, yes, but in doing so she had also placed herself in the role of caretaker of his bound-to-be irresponsible ways.

Elly sighed, her sympathies with Alastair since she could see the hurt in his eyes. ''Look, dearest,'' she began gently, taking hold of his arm with both hands,

"I can only try to understand how upset you must be by what you can only see as my *deplorable* lack of confidence in you, but—"

"I want the two of you moved to my estate in Surrey as soon as Leslie is able to travel," Alastair cut in abruptly, rising to pace back and forth in front of her as he spoke, his gaze directed at the carpet.

"What?" The question was all she could muster, for his commanding words had rendered her nearly bereft of speech.

"Please don't interrupt, pet. My mind is quite made up. I've already set things in motion. You should be able to leave before the week is out, according to Doctor Wallingsworth, if you take the trip in stages. I should have sent you two days ago, when I first learned Leslie was in danger, but you were ill. Then yesterday, when we seemed to come to an understanding, I couldn't bear to let you leave me. I was a selfish fool, but that is all over now. Your safety is my primary objective—everything else is secondary."

She stared up at him in amazement. "You—you want us to leave?"

He turned to face her. "I don't *want* you to leave. I'm telling you that you are leaving. It's the only way. Surely you can see that, darling?"

Elly shook her head. "No. No, I don't see that. Not unless you are prepared to leave as well. If we were all to go away, there would no longer be any reason for the spy to try to eliminate us, Captain Wiggins could set the trap you told me about, and everything would be over. But you're not planning to leave with us, are you, Alastair?"

He walked around the table to take hold of her upper arms. "Of course I'm not! What sort of coward do you think I am? Is your estimation of me still so low? A spy is operating from *my* beaches, Elly. Not content with that, he is also doing his damnedest to rid the world of every last Earl of Hythe. I'm not about to leave his capture up to the Lieutenant Fishbournes of this world. This is a personal fight. He's *mine,* Elly—and I'm going to be a part of his downfall!''

Elly had never seen him so serious, never seen him without a twinkle in his eyes or a smile on his lips. This was a new Alastair Lowell, and one who frightened her even as he thrilled her. She put her hands on his chest. "What are you planning, Alastair? Surely you're not going to—"

"Lieutenant Fishbourne ter see you, ma'am," Iris interrupted quietly from the doorway. "He said ter tell yer he used the knocker this time. Should I tell him yer busy? Yer sure as check look busy ter me. Good mornin', m'lor—sir.''

Alastair's grip on her upper arms tightened for a moment. "Alastair?" she asked, searching his face for some hint of how she should proceed. "What shall I do?''

His smile flashed white between the golden whiskers of his beard. The Alastair Lowell she had fallen in love with was back. Yet, she saw, his eyes weren't shining with humor. They were glinting silver-grey with determination.

"Do, my pet?" he answered softly, rubbing her cheek with the back of his fingers. "I should think you would follow your heart. I'll be outside on the porch, as I would rather not face the good Lieutenant at the moment.''

Elly's hands fell to her sides as Alastair took two steps back, turned smartly on his heels, and walked quickly through the open doorway to the porch.

"Ma'am?"

She closed her eyes in confusion. What was she to do? How had she been put in this untenable position? It would be so easy to turn to Lieutenant Fishbourne, confess exactly what had been going on at Seashadow—tell him of Alastair's existence and the attempts on Leslie's life—and deliver responsibility for the capture of the spy-cum-murderer into the lap of the Preventive Officer.

But what would that do to Alastair—to them both? How could she profess to love him if she didn't trust him to protect his own? How could he love her if she showed so little faith in him?

"Ma'am, I'm needed in the kitchens. I'll jist tell the Lieutenant I couldn't find yer."

"No!" Elly ordered, whirling to face the young girl. "That won't be necessary. Please, Iris, show the Lieutenant in at once."

She sat down behind the tea tray and willed her hands not to shake as she poured herself a cup of tea, only spilling a few grains of sugar as she added a full two teaspoonsful to the dark, steaming liquid.

"Lieutenant Fishbourne, ma'am," Iris announced from the doorway, and the soldier strode into the drawing room, his hat tucked beneath his arm.

"Good day to you, Miss Dalrymple," he said, not bothering to sit down. "Thank you for seeing me. I can only stop for a moment, as I have pressing matters to attend to in Hythe."

"Good day to you, Lieutenant," Elly returned,

happy to hear that her voice was not shaking as she looked up at the tall blonde man. His skin was slightly flushed, and he looked almost human. "You appear to be excited. Would these pressing matters possibly have something to do with the spy who has been operating in the area?"

She watched as his expression became grim, inwardly moaning as she feared he was going to launch into another of his overly patriotic, dry-as-dust dissertations. "That they do, ma'am, but I am afraid I am not at liberty to discuss them with civilians. You understand, don't you, Miss Dalrymple?"

Elly smiled, taking a sip of tea. "Indeed yes, Lieutenant," she assured him brightly. "We females have no head for intrigue anyway. Oh! I just thought of something. You aren't here to cry off from my dinner invitation, are you? That would be too bad, for Mr. Bates is *so* eager to meet you."

She thought she heard something—some slight choking noise coming from the porch—but the Lieutenant didn't react. Elly took a deep breath and pinned her smile more firmly on her face.

He sat down gingerly, on the very end of the chair across from her. "As I am eager to meet him, ma'am," he vowed in earnest tones. "But, alas, duty prevents me from participating in what I am sure would have been a very entertaining evening. I would have sent round my apologies, but I wished to explain my reasons to you in person. Is your brother the Earl about?"

"Leslie?" The question surprised her, as he had never before asked to be introduced to her brother.

Surely word of his injury could not have traveled so quickly. "Why do you ask?"

He hopped to his feet, pulling on his gloves. "No reason, really," he answered lightly. "I had just wished to warn him that we've had word of poachers operating in the area, and I shouldn't like to think either you or the Earl could accidently stumble across a pack of the scoundrels in the woods. It is enough that my men are out there. But you can warn him for me, I imagine. You won't forget, will you, ma'am?"

"As I *forgot* to tell you about Mr. Bates, Lieutenant?"

"Exactly," he agreed with a smile, making Elly long to box his ears. Obviously his opinion of women was not high. How he must have regretted his initial impulse to enlist her in his cause. "Well, I must be going. There is no limit to my work this day, but tonight should prove to be the end of it. Please, Miss Dalrymple, keep away from the beach for one more day, no matter if you hear shouts, or shots, or whatever."

Elly carefully placed the teacup on the platter and rose to walk over to where Fishbourne stood. "There is something very important going on, isn't there, Lieutenant? Are you expecting that terrible spy—or some smugglers—to come ashore at Seashadow tonight? How terribly—" she searched for an adequately "female" word "—terribly *exciting!* I should like above all things to see this fearsome group in shackles. You are so *brave,* Lieutenant! How I envy you men your perilous exploits, not that I should ever wish such a dangerous experience for myself."

There was another sound from the porch—and this

was definitely a low rumble of male laughter—so that she quickly coughed delicately, to cover the sound.

She watched as the Lieutenant pulled himself up very straight, the sun streaming through the open doorway glinting off the shiny metal buttons of his uniform jacket. "It is all in the course of my work, Miss Dalrymple," he said with, she supposed, his impression of manly modesty. "You and the Earl—and Mr. Bates, of course—will stay clear of the beach until you hear from me again, won't you?"

Elly pressed her clasped hands to her breast. "I should think so! And then, perhaps, when this horrid business is over, you shall consent to be guest of honor at a celebratory dinner here at Seashadow?"

"I should be honored, ma'am," Fishbourne told her, bowing. "Good day, ma'am."

He had just regained the foyer when a slight sound—the one she had previously recognized as suppressed laughter—reached her clearly from the porch, and she turned to see Alastair walking into the room, his hands applauding softly.

"I hear Mrs. Siddons is about to retire, pet," he told her, coming over to plant a kiss on her cheek. "If we were to quarrel and you should cry off from our engagement, I do believe you have quite a future treading the boards. 'You are so *brave*, Lieutenant!' That was the absurd, posturing idiot you wished to entrust with our safety? I wouldn't be surprised if half the village shows up on the beach tonight, if that was an example of how well the man keeps a secret. I can only thank my own good sense for keeping the fact of my existence safely from him."

Elly sat down, putting one hand to her forehead, for

she had developed quite a headache. "Don't tease me, Alastair," she warned tersely. "I did what you wanted, didn't I? Now, tell me what you are going to do. It is definitely tonight, isn't it? This isn't just an ordinary smuggling run. The spy is going to try to leave England tonight. That is why the Lieutenant had to cry off his invitation to dinner."

"The good Lieutenant has other duties tonight, yes," Alastair answered, sitting down beside her. "I received a little missive from Geoffrey confirming the event only an hour ago."

"He warned you to stay away from the beach tonight?" Elly asked hopefully, knowing she wasn't going to like his answer.

"Yes, pet," she heard Alastair say, and her heart plummeted to her toes. "That is exactly right. It would seem that the good Captain is very concerned for my welfare. Poor Geoffrey."

"RICE. RICE! Where the devil is the fellow? This is no time to be answering a call to nature! O'Brien— find Rice, now!"

"Softly, my friend, softly," Alastair warned congenially, sliding into the shallow, hollowed-out ditch the Captain had made in the sand some thirty yards to the left of the spot the smugglers had last used to land their boat. "Rice won't be coming, Geoffrey. He is, um, all tied up right now. But not to worry. He kindly loaned me his cloak before he left, so I can just take his place."

"Lord Hythe!" the Captain rasped, recognizing the voice of the Earl even if he couldn't see the man's face in the darkness. "You didn't!"

"Ah, Geoff, but I did. You knew I would, deep in your heart of hearts. Admit it, man, and let us move on to more important matters. Where is our genuine spy? Safely tucked away in some guardhouse hours ago, I suppose, before I could safely slip away from Seashadow. Good work. I like your hat, by the by, even if it is a bit large. I suppose it keeps you from having to rub lampblack on your head to keep down the shine? It's called a sailor's toque, isn't it—the headgear, that is. Yes, it's very attractive, Geoff."

"Yes, it is, and thank you," the Captain muttered, shaking his head so that the large, drooping knitted cap slipped down over one eye. "What on earth am I thanking you for!" he exploded, which was difficult to do, as he knew he had to keep his voice low. "My lord, you would try a saint, and that is someone I most definitely am not! But you wanted to know about the spy, didn't you? We intercepted him three hours ago, on the road. Impertinent young fellow by the name of Bunk. Now what, sir?"

"You know what I want, don't you, Geoffrey? I fully intend to sail away on that boat—that is the smuggler's boat signaling to us, isn't it? Don't you think they're expecting some sort of answer from their passenger? You only gave me a broad outline of your plan, remember."

Captain Wiggins rolled his rotund body onto his back—reminding Alastair of a turtle tipped onto its shell—angling his head for a better view of the dark waters of the Channel.

There was no moon and it was as dark as the inside of a pig's bladder, so that it was nearly impossible to miss the flashes of light emanating from the lantern that one of the smugglers was alternately covering and uncovering, obviously in hopes of receiving an answering signal from the beach.

"O'Brien, flash the bloody lantern!" Captain Wiggins whispered the harsh command as Alastair—who had already recognized the rather anonymous-looking shadows to be no less than ten soldiers, who were scattered about the beach and dug into shallow ditches just like their Captain—concentrated on the movements of the smuggler's craft.

"Probably busy scratching at a flea," Alastair observed charitably, as at the moment he was engaged in a similar pursuit. "Ah, there it is. Good show, O'Brien," he called quietly across the sand.

"This is not a game, sir," Wiggins pointed out through clenched teeth.

"Indeed, no, Geoffrey," Alastair agreed quickly. "I should say it isn't. I trust that tomorrow you will allow me a few minutes alone with our spy before you ship him to London? I want to be sure he is the man I'm after—just so that all the ends are neatly tied, if you know what I mean. Now, if you'll be so kind as to give me the papers, I shall be on my way to The Cold Heart and the lovely Yvette. It may not be good form to keep a fellow spy waiting."

Wiggins looked toward the Channel, to see that a small rowboat was heading toward the beach, with two strapping men at the oars. It was either move now or lose the entire project. But how would he explain this change of plans in London—especially if the Earl bollixed the mission and ended up at the bottom of the sea with his throat cut? Yet, the Captain considered further, as the Earl was already supposed to be dead—what difference would it make anyway?

"Geoff," Alastair prodded, "the papers, if you please. My excuse to Miss Dalrymple for coming out tonight was unbelievably lame, and she's as suspicious as a wife whose husband has suddenly started walking around the house smiling and whistling. You wouldn't want her showing up here, now would you?"

The Captain reached inside his jacket and pulled out a fat packet in oilskin. "You'll be careful, won't you, sir?"

"Why, Geoff, I didn't know you cared so much." Alastair reached across the sand to pull off the Captain's toque and plant a smacking kiss on the man's bald pate. "You will tell the men to shoot over my head, won't you? Thank you so much. See you at dawn, my friend. I would appreciate it greatly if you were not late."

"Lieutenant Fishbourne and his men are most probably already at sea, ready to follow at a safe distance, and we'll be doing likewise the moment you are safely gone," Wiggins assured him as Alastair rose, pulling the hood of the black cloak down over his face. "You'll never be completely alone."

"How that comforts me, Geoffrey," Alastair told him, only slightly mollified, as he was not unaware that he was embarking on a very dangerous mission. The two pistols he had tucked into his waistband, and the very long knife that was concealed in his boot, added only marginally to his assurance. "I've had one nocturnal encounter with the cold waters of the Channel and do not relish a second."

"They've took the bait and landed, Captain," came

a whisper from the darkness. "Is Rice movin' his arse this night or not, d'ya know?"

"He's moving," Alastair whispered back, drawing one of the pistols from his waistband and brandishing it in the air. He began to run down to the shoreline at full tilt, spouting unintelligible French while being careful to keep his face averted as he pointed the pistol behind him and fired.

The bark of ten firearms going off nearly at once was all but deafening, the flash of the guns splitting the dark night with red fire and smoke.

A heartbeat later the fire was being returned from the rowboat as Alastair ran, his cloak flying out behind him, his boots kicking up loose stones and sand. He could feel bullets whizzing past him—at least one of them coming close enough to give credence to his haste in flinging himself face-first into the rowboat and yelling, *"Se presser, vous! Se presser!"* which was rather inelegant French for "Get a move on!"

Clambering to the front of the boat, Alastair missed the thin wooden bench and inadvertently sat himself down in the very bottom of the boat, wetting himself thoroughly in the fetid seawater that sloshed inside as the bow cut into the waves, the oarsmen straining to reach the speedy Dutch dogger that was already weighing anchor.

"Shut yer froggie mouth an' git yer bleedin' carcass outta m'way so's Oi kin ter this oar better," one of the smugglers ordered, kicking at Alastair's feet. "Else they'll be off an' leavin' us behind fer gallows bait."

Wiggins and his men were standing at the water's edge now, still firing, but already their shots were falling short. Alastair looked forward to see hands reaching for him, to rudely hoist him onto the deck of the Dutch dogger, a ship that was probably swifter than whatever slug of a boat Lieutenant Fishbourne would be using to follow them.

He was leaving England, leaving his beloved Elly, with only a slight hope of ever seeing either one of them again. It really was quite oppressive, being a man of honor.

"Wot in bloody blue blazes happened?" a very large, bearded man demanded, grabbing Alastair roughly by the shoulder and whipping him around so that he had to lower his head to keep his face hidden. The hand remained on his shoulder, the strong fingers squeezing viselike until Alastair's arm went numb. "Oi don't like this. There weren't apposed ter be no troubles. This'll cost yer, froggie!"

Alastair was a born gambler, and he gambled now, with his life as the stakes. He savagely hit the large man's hand away and growled, "Unhand me, Englisher, and go about your business. You weel be paid. Feel-thy *cochon*. Do you wish for to talk, or do you wish for to have ze gold in ze pockets?"

The man grunted, raising a closed fist, then seemed to think better of it and moved away, turning back to warn gruffly, "But I'm tellin' yer now, froggie, this here is the last trip yer'll be makin' with Blackie Baxter. Yer musta bin gettin' careless, that's wot. Oi'd druther end m'days in a bleedin' jail."

"I only hope I can accommodate you, Blackie," Alastair murmured under his breath, finding himself a dry, out-of-the-way corner where he would sit, rub his sore shoulder, and ride out the hours until they landed in France.

CHAPTER NINE

ELLY WATCHED, one hand pressed to her mouth so that she wouldn't cry out, as Alastair ran across the width of the beach to the sea, bullets flying over his head. She continued to crouch at the crest of the hill, her dark brown merino cape concealing her trembling figure, as the rowboat made its rendezvous with the larger smuggler craft.

Only when the dogger had begun to move out to sea and the soldiers on the beach turned to climb back up the hill did she speak. "Captain Wiggins? Yoo-hoo!" she began tentatively. "Don't shoot me, please. This is Elinor Dalrymple speaking. Which one of you is Captain Geoffrey Wiggins?"

"Criminy! Who's that?" O'Brien asked his commanding officer. "It sounds like a woman. And what would a woman be doin' here, Captain, d'ye think? Do ye knows her?"

"And that's just what I needed—the suspicious fiancée," Wiggins muttered under his breath, allowing O'Brien to help him up the steep incline until he was standing face-to-face with Elly. "His lordship didn't think he had fooled you, ma'am," he said without preamble, puffing slightly from his recent exertion. "Luckily, I think he did succeed in pulling the wool over the smugglers' eyes."

Elly squinted through the darkness to get a better look at the Captain, whose short, rotund frame would have inspired her confidence had he been her vicar, or even the village baker. He did not, she decided, cut half so imposing a figure as Lieutenant Fishbourne. Yet she immediately felt she could trust him with her life—and Alastair's life—not that her fiancé's reckless heroics had given her much choice.

"Where is Lieutenant Fishbourne, Captain?" she asked, searching the faces of the other soldiers and not finding that of the Preventive Officer.

"Fishbourne? How did you—oh, never mind," Captain Wiggins said, shaking his toque-covered head. "I should be used to it by now. Tell me, ma'am, is there anything Lord Hythe neglected to tell you?"

Elly smiled. "You like him too, don't you, Captain?" she said, falling into step with the man as they walked toward the path that led to the small pier where she had earlier spotted a black-painted Coast Guard yawl.

"Yes, ma'am, that I do," Geoffrey Wiggins admitted, offering his elbow to Elly, as the path was strewn with small rocks. "I only hope he can carry this off." He called back over his shoulder, "O'Brien—have you found Rice yet? It would serve him right if we left him tied up in some dank cave the whole night long, but I need him to escort Miss Dalrymple back to Seashadow."

"On the contrary, Captain," Elly corrected quietly. "I shan't need Mister Rice's accompaniment at all— as I shall be sailing with you. That's very ingenious, you know, painting the yawl black. Are the sails black as well? You are sailing, aren't you?"

The Captain stopped abruptly in the middle of the path, so that one of the soldiers nearly cannoned into his back. "You want to go with us on the yawl? That is totally out of the question, ma'am! I cannot allow you to put yourself in danger."

Wiggins's small outburst wasn't lost on his men. "A woman 'board ship, Captain?" the man directly behind him questioned, obviously horrified. "Say it ain't so, sir. We'll have bad luck fer sure." His mates, all breaking into agitated chatter, seemed to agree with him.

Elly, however, had figured on just such a reaction, and so was prepared for their protests. Reaching into the voluminous pocket of her cape, she withdrew an ugly-looking pistol she had coerced Mrs. Biggs into liberating from the locked gun cabinet at Seashadow.

Poking the business end of the thing into Captain Wiggins's soft belly, she said tersely, "I think you should convince your men that they are mistaken, Captain. Deciding to leave a woman—this woman in particular—onshore holds twice the danger of taking her aboard ship."

Wiggins looked down at the pistol—noting that it was, indeed, cocked—and raised his hands above his head. No wonder she and the Earl got on like a house on fire. They were both mad as hatters. "Now, ma'am," he began nervously, "don't you think this is going too far? I mean, the smugglers are getting farther and farther out to sea with each passing moment, with only Lieutenant Fishbourne and his men in pursuit. We don't have time for this foolishness."

Elly was so nervous, she could feel the heavy pistol shaking in her two-handed grasp. "As you already know Alastair's destination, Captain, and do not intend to stop the smugglers' ship until they are away from the French shore and once more safely in English waters, I fail to see the rush. But you are right—we are wasting time. I suggest you order your men to go ahead and raise the mainmast and jiggermast, so that we can be on our way. The breeze is fresh, but we cannot depend on it lasting.''

''Mizzenmast.''

Elly leaned slightly to her left to better hear the man who had spoken. ''What?''

''It's not a jiggermast, ma'am,'' O'Brien told her, reaching swiftly across her to knock the pistol harmlessly to the ground. ''A mizzenmast is what it is, don't you know. Captain? Are ye ready now, or are ye goin' ta stand here jawin' all the night long?''

How could she have been so stupid—so careless! Elly grabbed on to the Captain's arm, ready to beg him to allow her aboard ship. She knew she had been overreaching herself to threaten the man with a pistol, but she just had to be on that yawl when it set out to sea. Alastair might need her. Besides, she would go insane if she had to stay behind and wait for someone to come to Seashadow in the morning and tell her that he had been shot, or worse. ''Captain Wiggins—'' she began tearfully.

''Is it all right ye are, Captain?'' O'Brien interrupted, bending to pick up the pistol. ''Ye looked as nervous as a dog around an Irishman's boot for a minute there, if I do say so m'self.'' The soldier chuckled and shook his head. ''Jiggermast. It's the same thing as a mizzenmast, ain't it?''

The Captain was looking at Elly assessingly. ''Do

you know what I mean, Miss Dalrymple, when I say the word 'abaft'?''

A glimmer of hope invading her chest, Elly nodded furiously and answered, ''I've been reading about ships all my life, Captain Wiggins, as I have always known I would love the sea. That's why we came to Seashadow first, you know, so that I could be near the sea. But I'm babbling, aren't I? Abaft on a ship is aft—to the rear or stern. Is that where you'd like me to sit?'' she ended hopefully.

Wiggins sighed. ''I'd like you to sit in your parlor, ma'am, knitting socks. But if you were to sit very quietly—allowing O'Brien here to guard your pistol— I think you might come along with us. The way this night has been going—and when my superiors hear of it, I wouldn't be surprised to find myself guarding a lighthouse at John O'Groat's—I may as well be hung for a sheep as a lamb.''

Wiggins found himself being kissed for the second time in a half hour, a very disconcerting circumstance for the crusty bachelor, and within a few minutes the yawl was heading into the open water, Elly perched primly on a barrel of gunpowder, her brown merino cape wrapped decorously about her ankles.

A WOMAN NAMED Yvette should be blonde, Alastair thought meanly, nursing his mug of inferior wine. Blonde and petite—and with a dimple in her chin. Besides, she was a spy, and a spy—or least a female spy—should be glamorous.

His Yvette, however, was tall and dark and of an indeterminate age, and her chin sported not a dimple but a large wart shaped much like the island of Sicily—with a single black hair growing out of it. When she smiled, which the unfortunate woman did often, it was to show a mouth sadly lacking in teeth.

But he had not come to France for romance, Alastair reminded himself, tipping back the last of his wine and waving his hand for Yvette to approach with another mug. As she plunked the thing down on the wooden tabletop, sloshing some of it onto the scarred surface, he reached into his pocket to extract the thick packet of papers Wiggins had given him and pointedly placed it on the barmaid's tray.

"There had better be more in your pocket than that," Yvette gritted in gutter French, giving the packet a dismissing look. "But you are a pretty one, aren't you? Maybe you can pay me another way."

Alastair was nonplussed. He looked down at the packet, then toward the door, counting to be sure he had sat at the second table. Yes, he was in the right seat. Had he read the faded sign outside the tavern correctly? Christ on a crutch—was he in the wrong tavern…and with a pocketful of English gold but without a single French coin among them?

Smiling up at the barmaid as he replaced the packet in his jacket, he fought down his distaste and sudden apprehension to croon in what he hoped was equally fractured French, "*Ma petite chou!* I am so sorry, *mamselle*. I have come lately from Paris with this information for Yvette. I was told she was the prettiest barmaid at The Cold Heart—so when I saw you, *ma petit,* I naturally assumed—"

The barmaid turned her head to one side and spit at the floor. "Yvette!" she exclaimed. "Always it is Yvette! No one wants Berthe. Ah! *Quand on parle du loup, on en voit la queue!* Speak of the wolf and you see his tail! There is your Yvette, *m'sieur.* I wish you joy of her—and may you catch the pox!''

Berthe flounced away as Alastair leaned back in the chair, perspiration breaking out on his forehead as he watched the barmaid standing deep in conversation with another woman, the two of them looking over at him as they spoke.

The second woman, a small blonde whose major claim to beauty was nearly completely exposed by her low-cut peasant blouse, approached the table, her green eyes narrowed to slits. ''I am Yvette. Who are you? And where is Emeri, *m'sieur?''* she asked quietly. ''He promised me a pair of woolen drawers on his return. I want my drawers.''

Woolen drawers? Alastair repeated mentally, racking his brain in an effort to understand why the barmaid would want woolen underwear? Why not something pretty—like a shawl, or jewelry, or silken cloth? The answer hit him just as swiftly. England got those things from *this* side of the Channel. Woolen underwear, a mundane but useful product, was strictly an English invention.

Be that as it may, he did not have the dratted woman's drawers, damn the forgetful Emeri, who hadn't been carrying them—or else Wiggins most certainly would have given them to him.

''I know nothing of such things,'' he told her gruffly, reaching into his pocket once more for the packet. If he didn't get moving soon, the tide would turn, and he wouldn't put it past Blackie Baxter to leave him behind onshore. ''Mine is an extra trip.

Emeri had to stay over there a while longer—he should be back any time. Here.''

Yvette gave an elegant French shrug—for the divisions of class faded into nothingness when it came to a Frenchman's use of his or her body to express emotion. "You do not lie very well, *m'sieur*. I'll take English gold instead. If I cannot be warm this winter, at least I will not starve. The Little Corporal is doomed, and Yvette must take care of herself.''

She knew! The doxy knew! Alastair leaned forward. "What gave me away?'' he whispered, for if he was about to be hauled outside and hanged from the nearest lamppost, he felt he deserved to know what he had done to betray himself.

Yvette picked up the packet, then withdrew a single folded sheet of paper from her bodice and laid it on the table. "The gold, Englisher,'' she prompted, holding out her hand until Alastair laid a small bag of coins in her palm.

"Emeri is my pig of a husband, *m'sieur*—over there, behind the bar,'' she told him, quickly placing the bag where the paper had so recently resided and tucking the packet in her apron pocket. "The man who was supposed to be here tonight is Leonard, my lover. You will hang him, no? No matter. He was cheating on me with Berthe anyway. But I did so want the woolen drawers. Go now, Englisher, before you catch a fly in that mouth of yours.''

ELLY WAS CHILLED through to the bone, her teeth chattering uncontrollably as she sat huddled on the keg of gunpowder, her eyes constantly searching the darkness for some sign of the Dutch dogger that was carrying Alastair.

The night had been interminable, both because of her fears for her beloved and due to the rapidly dawning realization that, although she might love the sea, her stomach obviously did not.

Captain Wiggins's yawl had made its rendezvous with Lieutenant Fishbourne's larger cutter several hours before, about five miles off the coast of Calais. The number of men and guns aboard the cutter did much to comfort Elly, although she sincerely hoped the smugglers would decide against making a fight of it.

The cutter had sent over a longboat for Captain Wiggins, who had spent at least an hour on the larger ship with Fishbourne, surely discussing strategy before returning to the yawl to tell Elly that so far everything was going according to their plans and it would all be over shortly.

She pulled her cape more firmly around her, her left hand clutching the belaying pin she had appropriated for use as a club when no one was looking. She didn't want a fight, but she knew she should be ready for one. And this time she wouldn't make the mistake of being distracted, so that she could be unarmed without a struggle.

Surely Geoffrey Wiggins's definition of "shortly" could not be the same as hers. What was taking so long? It would soon be light, and the smugglers would discover that Alastair wasn't their regular passenger. Were they in the right spot? The Channel was so very large—much larger than Elly had supposed. How could Captain Wiggins and Lieutenant Fishbourne be so sure that they would even be close enough to *see* the smugglers' boat as it went by on its way back to England, yet alone capture it?

So much seemed to depend on luck. This had to be the most ridiculous, farfetched, *impossible* plan in the history of man! Oh, why did the yawl have to pitch so—her stomach was so queasy!

"Would ye be wantin' a bit of good Irish whiskey, ma'am, jist ta take the chill outta yer bones?" O'Brien asked, coming up to her, a small tin flask in his hand. "Captain Wiggins wouldn't have ta know."

The idea was very tempting. Elly eyed the flask, then looked down the deck to where the Captain was standing, his back to her. "Thank you, Mister O'Brien," she said, reaching out her hand.

"It's jist O'Brien, ma'am," the soldier corrected her. "I owes it to ye, after knockin' that barkin' iron outta ye hand. Ye sure are a spunky one. Me ma woulda loved ye. I didn't hurt ye any, did I? And don't ye be worritin' about his lordship. Old Bullie won't let nuthin' happen ta him."

"Old Bullie?" Elly questioned, coughing slightly as the heat of the whiskey burned the back of her throat. "Oh, you mean Captain Wiggins, don't you?" Her eyes were stinging from the potency of the drink, but already she could feel its warmth penetrating and easing her frozen limbs.

O'Brien took back the flask, turned to see if his superior was watching, and quickly lifted it to his mouth to take a long pull of its contents. "And who else would I be meanin', ma'am, if not him? He's the best, ma'am. Glory be, and the stories I could tell ye— uh-oh!" The soldiers were beginning to bustle about the small craft, some manning the black sails, the rest holding their firearms at the ready. "If ye'll excuse me, ma'am, I think the dogger has come out to play."

Elly jumped up to grab O'Brien's arm. "What will happen now? How will Wiggins get the Earl off the smugglers' boat?"

O'Brien leaned back against the side of the yawl, his eyes scanning the horizon, and his rifle at the ready, but seemingly not disobliged to talk. "It's nearly daybreak, so we'll soon be in plain sight. We're two against one. Fishy will shoot a round across the dogger's bow. That oughta do it, and the dogger will heave to—unless the Gentlemen want ta try ta make a run for it."

What little Elly knew about the smugglers had led her to believe they were a desperate, coldhearted bunch, capable of anything. "But if they do decide to make a run for it, Mister O'Brien?" Elly asked, her heart pounding as she saw the speed with which the bow of the dogger was cutting through the water. "Lieutenant Fishbourne's vessel seems to fairly bristle with cannon, but surely he won't use them—not with the Earl aboard. It would be too dangerous."

The soldier lifted his cap to scratch his head. "Now ye got me, ma'am. I doesn't know wot we'll do iffen the dogger runs. I guess his lordship will jist hafta get himself wet, and swim for it."

The next ten minutes were the longest Elly had ever lived through as she watched the three boats maneuver in the choppy seas as the slowly rising sun lightened the sky. Finally the cutter was no more than a hundred yards from the dogger, and Elly strained her ears to listen for Lieutenant Fishbourne's order for the smugglers to strike their sails.

The order never came. As Elly watched, her heart in her throat, the dogger, definitely the faster of the two ships, began to move away.

Captain Wiggins began to jump up and down on the deck of the yawl, his toque in his hands, waving his short arms furiously and shouting to Fishbourne at the top of his lungs. "The bow, man!" he yelled frantically. "Shoot across their bow!"

A premature dawn exploded upon the water in the form of a full broadside from the cutter, an avalanche of shot crashing through the rigging of the dogger and ripping a gaping hole in the port side just at the water line.

"It's sinking!" Elly screamed while O'Brien, cursing under his breath, held her back, as it appeared she was about to leap over the side. She searched the debris-filled water frantically, praying for some sign of Alastair as the men aboard the dogger abandoned the rapidly sinking boat. "There—there he is!" she cried at last, pointing to a large black cloak that was floating atop the water. "Quickly, O'Brien! Quickly! Do something. We must save him!"

"I KNOW YOU MUST think me a sorry enough looking shrimp, Hugo," Alastair remarked, fighting back a groan as he waved his friend off and stepped, naked, onto the carpet, "but I promise you, I can still get myself out of a tub. Stop twittering over me like an old cockerel with a prize pullet."

"*Aaarrgh, aaarrgh,*" the giant answered, gently

wrapping a large white bath sheet around his master's bruised and battered form.

"Thank you, my friend," Alastair said, moving to sit down on the edge of the bed, wondering how anyone could hurt so much and still be alive. "I am not sure what you said, but if I might recommend something to you—don't ever get blown up. It hurts like the very devil."

A half hour later, and against Hugo's unintelligible but vigorous protests, Alastair was on his way downstairs to face Elly—who he was sure was just waiting for him to show his face, biding her time to be sure that he would live, just so she could kill him.

What a night he'd had, he thought, leaning heavily on the cane he had once used in jest as he made his way haltingly to the drinks cabinet and poured himself a liberal three fingers of brandy. Between the explosions and Elly's coldly efficient care of his wounds once Wiggins had retrieved him from the sea—by the ignominious use of a grappling hook—he didn't know whether he would have preferred being a dead hero to his current condition.

Elly was livid, there was no denying it, but he wasn't so knocked about in his head that he was going to allow her more than five minutes of lecturing before he reminded her that she had been on the yawl—which wasn't exactly an innocent act.

He looked around the room, lighted by the late afternoon sun, wishing Elly would make her entrance, ring a peal over his head, and forgive him—for they still had a lot to talk about.

"There you are, Alastair. I may not yet be your wife and you may think I am overstepping myself to make demands on you, but you are to never, I say, *never* do anything like that again!''

He turned to face the doorway, a smile on his face. Bless her, she was right on time. ''Good afternoon, my love. Don't you look all the crack. Parliament should pass a law stating that you must always wear your hair down. But you said something, didn't you? I was mentally counting my bruises, I'm afraid—as well as being hampered by this ringing in my ears that has not gone away since Lieutenant Fishbourne did his reenactment of Vesuvius erupting—and was not really attending. Was it anything important?''

''Oh, Alastair, I can't do it! I can't rage at you, even if I should!'' she cried, running across the room to launch herself into his arms—a move he would have enjoyed immensely if it weren't for the fact that his ribs ached abominably. ''You were so brave, and I was so afraid. Please, my darling, no more heroics. I don't believe I could endure it.''

He patted her on the back, happy she couldn't see his smile. ''Pish tosh, pet, don't turn into a watering pot on me now—not after you've been brave to the point of idiocy, following me to sea like that. Besides, how can you really see me if you have your face crushed against my chest? Don't tell me you didn't notice, my darling. I have a surprise for you.''

Pulling back fractionally in his arms, Elly looked up to see that Alastair was clean-shaven. ''Oh,'' she exclaimed, reaching up to stroke his cheek, ''you're even prettier than I'd imagined, although it will take some getting used to, I suppose. After all, I shan't be able to become angry with you and call you a great hairy brute anymore, shall I? I love you, Alastair.''

''As I love you, pet.'' He leaned down to kiss her lightly on the nose, neatly disengaging her arms from around his waist before he so unmanned himself as to wince with the pain she was unconsciously providing. ''I don't remember you ever calling me a great hairy brute,'' he commented a moment later, leading her to the settee so that he could sit down before he fell down.

''You probably never heard me,'' she told him, taking hold of both his hands as if she were afraid he would disappear if she let him go, ''but I have called you several things, I'm afraid—many of which you were most unfortunately present to hear. I could have employed my time more wisely by thinking up horrible things to say about that terrible, bumbling Fishy.''

''Fishy?''

Elly nodded vigorously. ''Lieutenant Fishbourne. That's what Mister O'Brien calls him, so that I hardly think he's popular with the men. They call Captain Wiggins Old Bullie, but with him I'm sure it's a term of affection. Anyway, Mister O'Brien is one of the soldiers. He's the one who knocked the pistol from my hand when I was threatening Captain Wiggins with it so that he would take me aboard the yawl with him. And he gave me some whiskey when I was cold.'' She moved even closer to Alastair's side, squeezing his hands. ''Darling, I've been thinking—''

''Yes, you've been—wait a minute!'' Alastair sat up straight, looking down at Elly, his eyes wide. ''You held a *pistol* on Geoffrey? Geoffrey *Wiggins?*'' No wonder she had been so quick to forgive him for lying to her about his involvement with the capture of the spy and the smugglers. It would appear that the demure, ladylike love of his life had been up to her pretty little chin in some rather questionable activities of her own. "And just who was it who gave you whiskey— Wiggins or this O'Brien fellow?"

She let go of his hands and faced front on the settee. "It doesn't matter," she said dismissingly. "What matters is that Lieutenant Fishbourne disobeyed orders. I thought the Captain was going to have an apoplexy! Fishy was supposed to shoot a single cannonball across the bow of the smugglers' boat—not sink it with a full broadside."

Alastair leaned back with a smile on his face as he replied idly, "Geoffrey explained it to me. Fishbourne's men misunderstood his order and fired all the cannon instead of just the one. You held a pistol on Geoffrey—and *threatened* him?" he ended, his head still reeling as he mentally pictured Elly pointing a pistol at Captain Wiggins.

Elly whirled about to face him. "Would you stop babbling about Captain Wiggins? *Yes,* I threatened him. I had to do *something.* I couldn't just watch you sail away, not knowing what would happen to you. Now—will you please listen to me?"

Alastair sat at attention, waggling his eyebrows. "Yes, ma'am," he said smartly, "anything you say, ma'am. After all, I wouldn't want you to shoot me or anything. What did you want me to hear?"

"I think Lieutenant Fishbourne didn't want anyone to get off that dogger alive," she announced gravely, lifting her chin as if daring him to contradict her. "And—to take my supposition a step farther—I think Captain Wiggins thinks so too. He expressly told me to tell you not to leave the house until he could finish with the smugglers who survived and come here—for a private conversation that had to do with your continued good health.''

Alastair's smile disappeared as he gave Elly his full attention. ''A guilty man would wish to eliminate any evidence pointing to him, wouldn't he? But do I believe Fishbourne was involved with spying and smuggling? He's so full of patriotic speeches—and he didn't try to kill the real spy, did he? No, I don't think it's possible. It doesn't make sense. Did Wiggins say anything else?''

Elly shook her head. ''Everything was very rushed on the dock, what with you all but unconscious and many of the smugglers bleeding and shouting to wake the dead—but I did hear him say something strange. I didn't really understand what he meant.''

''Which was,'' Alastair prompted, the short hairs on the back of his neck beginning to prickle with a growing suspicion that would go a long way toward explaining Fishbourne's attack on the dogger.

Elly sighed. ''First you have to promise me you will stay inside until Captain Wiggins arrives. I don't think I could stand it if both you and Leslie were laid low by one of the 'poachers.' ''

''I promise, Elly,'' Alastair said impatiently, wondering why women always felt they had to have their men promise them things, when everybody knew a man could not really promise something when he didn't know if he could live up to it. ''Get on with it.''

''He said that it was beginning to look as if you had been right all along. He said it was crazy—but it was possible. Now, what could he have meant by that? You came here thinking that either Leslie or I had tried to kill you in order to get the title—and don't shake your head, because you and I both know it's true. But Wiggins couldn't possibly mean that he now believes that one of us is guilty—could he?''

Alastair stood, reaching for his cane, and began to pace the carpet, absently rubbing at his cleanly shaven chin. ''No, of course not, pet,'' he assured her, his mind racing as thought after thought hit him. ''Although it must have something to do with that first attempt on my life, if Geoff doesn't even want me out-of-doors. It seems impossible, but—''

''*Nothing* is impossible, Lowell, except that you seem to have more lives than a cat.''

Both Elly and Alastair turned at the sound of a male voice, directing their attention to the man who was standing just inside the open doors that led to the porch.

''Who in hell is—''

''Fishy!'' Elly exclaimed, answering Alastair's unfinished question. ''It can't be!''

The Lieutenant advanced into the room, a pistol in each hand. ''Cousin Jason, actually,'' he said punctiliously, ''although I had never heard of you or your brother until you showed up here at Seashadow, to ruin all my plans.''

Eyeing the uncocked pistols, Alastair moved slowly to his left, to shield Elly from the line of fire. ''Cousin Jason,'' he said affably, smiling wryly as he shook his head. ''So you're the one I have to thank for my dunk in the Channel? For *both* my dunks in the Channel, as a matter of fact. I wonder how many other relatives I have rattling about that I have never met. I cannot believe my parents were so remiss as not to mention both you and the Dalrymples. But then, now that I think of it, it appears the Dalrymples were a surprise to you as well.''

Fishbourne stopped walking, planting his feet a foot apart on the carpet, his hands steady as he visually inspected Alastair. ''You cannot know what it was like,'' he said quietly, as if to himself. ''I sat there in Hythe, day in, day out, waiting for word to come that I was the new Earl. I waited and waited. But nothing happened. Then one day I was ordered to come to Seashadow to tell the new Earl that his beaches were being used by smugglers.''

''You must have been devastated,'' Alastair commiserated, motioning for Elly to stand up and move behind him.

Fishbourne used the barrel of one pistol to scratch his temple. ''And what an Earl!'' he said in obvious distaste. ''The man is a complete fool. He bought those toadstools from me without a blink. Yet he's such a lucky fool—all my attempts on his life came so close, only to fail.''

''As you failed with your attempt on my life—although I must tell you that you do a commendable job when you try to blow up a boat,'' Alastair inserted, taking one small step forward, Elly nearly on his heels. ''When did you find out that I was still alive, Cousin Jason? I had expressly told Wiggins not to mention it to anyone.''

''When he came aboard the cutter last night,'' Fishbourne answered, his pale green eyes rather glazed, as if he still hadn't quite recovered from the shock of

Wiggins's disclosure and was acting more from impulse than design. "He told me to be especially careful, as you were the rightful Earl of Hythe and he'd have my liver and lights if any harm befell you."

"At which point you immediately decided to do me as much harm as possible," Alastair slid in, taking yet another step, Elly once again moving right along with him.

Fishbourne smiled, as if in agreement. "It came to me instantly that I would have to blow the entire dogger out of the water. Wiggins could never let it be known you had died *twice*. It would be too embarrassing for the War Office. There would be no real investigation."

"And then you could get back to the business of killing my brother," Elly piped up, stepping out from behind Alastair. "You are totally despicable, Lieutenant Fishbourne—as well as a very bad shot!"

"Elly, for God's sake, don't get him angry," Alastair whispered out of the corner of his mouth. "He's wavering, don't you see that? Let me handle him."

"Hallo!"

"Leslie!" Elly hissed, grabbing Alastair's upper arm at the exact spot where a large piece of the Dutch dogger's splintered deck had struck, bruising the entire area, causing Alastair to wonder who was going to kill him first, Fishbourne or his betrothed.

"Isn't it grand—I'm back on my feet again, nearly as good as new," Leslie trilled from the doorway. "Oh, it was all right, being in bed, and I did get a lovely drawing of my big toe—although the angle wasn't quite right—but I'm up now, and happy to be downstairs. I told you—the bullet touched nothing at all of importance. Well, are you both just going to stand there? Isn't anyone going to congratulate me? Oh, I say—isn't that fellow holding a pair of pistols?''

"Leslie, be quiet," Elly ordered, grabbing her brother as he made to pass by her, most probably to walk straight up to Jason Fishbourne and introduce himself. "This is Lieutenant Fishbourne. He is the man who tried to kill you."

Leslie didn't hesitate—he immediately took two steps to the rear and fell to the carpet, to cower behind his sister's skirts. "John, Elly—what is he going to do?"

Alastair—or John, as Leslie still called him—turned slightly to look at Elly. "Yes, Elly, what is he going to do? Do you have any suggestions for him? Poor Cousin Jason here has only two pistols—two bullets— and now there are three of us. It presents quite a dilemma for the poor fellow, doesn't it? Not that he could have shot any of us and still hoped to cheat the hangman and take his place as Earl in any case. No, I think Cousin Jason's visit is more spur-of-the-moment than planned, don't you?''

There was a sound at the doorway from the foyer, and a moment later a loud, angry roar shook the chandelier. "Correction," Alastair amended wryly, looking toward the door. "There are *four* of us. Hugo—be a good fellow, please, and don't startle the Lieutenant with any sudden movements."

The giant—his great hands balled into fists— stopped in the act of plunging across the room, his mouth working furiously as he moaned his frustration and concern.

Alastair could sense Fishbourne's mounting terror.

Nothing seemed to be going right for the man—what with not one but a pair of Earls who refused to co-operate and die, an inheritance that kept eluding him, an interfering lady who thwarted him at every turn, and a superior officer who was suspicious of his motives. A lesser man would have broken under the strain long ago.

For all the trouble the man had caused, Alastair found himself actually pitying the Lieutenant, who must have hatched his scheme within sight of Sea-shadow—within sight of what would have been his if not for an accident of birth.

Alastair took another step, holding out his hands. "Jason, it's over. Why don't you give me the pistols and we can all sit down and discuss our family tree? According to your cousin Elinor, we have more than our share of eccentrics hanging from the limbs. Was your father a gamester—or an artist? No? Perhaps a writer, then."

"He was an actor," Fishbourne spat, shakng his head. "A very bad actor. His father disowned him before I was born. But I am a Lowell—and I can prove it! If only those solicitors hadn't been so stupid! If only you had stayed dead! I'm a loyal English soldier. I have lived my whole life for my country. But what does my country do for me? It makes me stay in Hythe—where I can see all that I can't have. I deserve to succeed. I *deserve* Seashadow!"

Leslie peeked out from behind his sister's skirts. "I say, John, what is he talking about? He can't have Seashadow. It's mine. Elly—tell him it's mine."

"You don't deserve it!" Fishbourne shouted, stepping forward, both arms extended. Just as he was about to shoot, Alastair brought up his cane, knocking both pistols harmlessly out of the way.

Unfortunately this action badly unbalanced Alastair, and he found himself crumbling clumsily to his knees as Fishbourne turned to flee the way he had come—across the porch—while Elly cried anxiously, "Stop him! We can't let him get away—he might do something rash!"

"I'll give him something rash!" Alastair grumbled, picking up one of the pistols as he scrambled to his feet and broke into the best run his bruised body could muster. He got as far as the steps leading down to the lawns when he saw Jason Fishbourne, his back against a tree and Lily Biggs standing in front of him, her hands on his chest.

"Where was yer goin', Lieutenant?" Alastair heard the girl purr as she moved her hips closer to the wild-eyed soldier. "Was yer lookin' fer me? I told yer yer could see me any time yer liked. I have some news fer yer—about that John Bates who's bin livin' at Seashadow. Would yer like to know what it is? *Umm,* you're breathin' kinda heavy, ain't yer, Lieutenant? Mayhap yer'd like it iffen Lily opened some of these buttons, hmm, so's yer could cool off?"

Alastair walked up to the pair, the pistol leveled at Fishbourne's chest, and said, "Lily, I always knew you would come in handy one day—no matter that you were trying to bring me down. You saved me quite a run, and I thank you. Now be a good girl and step back, if you please. The Lieutenant doesn't have time for you right now."

"Yer—yer welcome, sir," Lily quavered, a new respectful tone in her voice. Then, her sky-blue eyes as wide as saucers as she continued to goggle at the pistol, she turned on her heels and ran for the safety of the kitchens as fast as she could, just as Hugo clapped a large paw on Fishbourne's shoulder and led the dazed man away.

"You were wonderful, darling," Elly said from somewhere behind him.

"Yes, stap me if he wasn't," Leslie agreed. "Absolutely wonderful. Tell me, Elly—what just happened?"

Dropping the pistol to the ground, Alastair opened his arms to Elly and they clung together, laughing until tears filled their eyes.

"And they say I'm strange," Leslie muttered to a butterfly that happened to be passing by. Then, since his sister and John Bates were kissing each other, he prudently took his leave.

EPILOGUE

"So, GEOFFREY, I imagine you'll be off on some other adventure now that things are all settled here?" Alastair asked, standing with his arm around his bride of two weeks. "I should like to go with you if circumstances were different, but I'm a married man now, you know, and very busy. As a matter of fact I wouldn't be surprised if I spent the remainder of my life drooling over the girl."

"Alastair!" Elly scolded, blushing. "Don't listen to him, Geoffrey. He only says things like that to shock people."

"No, I don't, pet," Alastair corrected, giving her trim waist a loving squeeze. "I only say things like that because my beautiful wife blushes to such advantage."

"Wretch," Elly responded, blushing in spite of herself.

"Wretch," he repeated, grinning. "Marriage being what it is, I can't understand why I waited so long to experience its delights. See how much she loves me, Geoff? The dear child fairly worships the ground I walk on."

"She also has been known to carry a pistol," the Captain warned, winking at Elly. "Well, I must be off.

I just wanted to stop by and tell you that you won't have to worry about Jason Fishbourne anymore.''

As she and Alastair walked arm in arm along the drive, Elly asked, ''He will be well treated in that asylum, won't he, Geoffrey? I feel rather sorry for him, actually, now that it's all behind us. Besides, if it hadn't been for Jason, Alastair and I would never have met.''

Captain Wiggins assured them that the Lieutenant was being well cared for and at last took his leave, glancing back as he was driven down the drive, waving to the newlywed couple.

''He's going, is he?'' Leslie said, coming up behind them, his clothing dusty and stuck with leaves, and a large cloth sack in his hands. ''That's too bad. I wanted to show him my latest discovery. John—would you like to see it?''

''Not John, Leslie,'' Elly corrected patiently. ''It's Alastair, remember? You're not the Earl anymore, but you are very happy about that because now you can spend all your time painting and creating and—Leslie, what do you have in that sack? It's moving!''

Leslie shifted the bag to one hand, striving to unlace the top. ''I'm not quite sure, Elly, actually. It looks rather like a cat, but its stripes are so odd. There are two large white ones—and they run down the entire length of its body. I say—where are you two off to now? Don't you want to see it either?''

Alastair, Elly's hand held tight in his as they scurried toward the house, called back over his shoulder, ''We just remembered we promised Hugo another lesson in printing his name. See you at dinner, Leslie, if you can make it—but please leave the 'cat' outside!''

Once they reached the safety of the foyer, Elly, whose sides ached from laughing, wrapped her arms around her waist and looked up at her husband. "Why didn't you tell him, Alastair? We'll probably have to bury the poor boy up to his neck in the gardens to rid him of the stink."

Alastair looked down at his wife and smiled. "Not only that, pet, but I doubt he'll be fit company for a week. Now, seeing that we most probably won't be disturbed—would you care to adjourn to our chamber? Hugo's lesson can wait, but I can think of *several* things I should delight in teaching you."

Smiling up into his eyes, Elly felt herself being lifted high in her husband's arms, and willingly accepted her fate.

"HAVE YOU HEARD the news?"

Lord Blakestone lowered his newspaper to glare overtop it at the young man who had dared to intrude on his peace. "You again!" he bellowed. "It seems you're always running in here, hot to tell us all something we'd rather not hear. What is it now?"

Hopwood refused to be cast down, for his news was particularly wonderful. "But—but I just heard. It's the most incredible thing! Lord Hythe is *alive!* And not only that, but he's a hero! He has captured a French spy, and an entire gang of smugglers, and—*and he's married!*"

Lord Blakestone stared at Hopwood until the young man was sure his lordship had succeeded in boring a hole clear through his brand-new canary waistcoat. "Indeed," the older man said at last. Turning to see that Lord Godfrey had just entered the room, he called out, "Freddie. I say, Freddie! This puppy says Wythe is alive. Didn't we just have a drink to mark his passing? Seems to me I paid for a wreath, too, come to think of it. And he's married to boot. How do you suppose he manages it?"

Hopwood, silently wondering what quirk in his makeup allowed him to continue to punish himself in this way, corrected wearily, "No, no, Lord Blackstone. Not Wythe—*Hythe*."

"Married, you say?" Lord Godfrey questioned, seating himself heavily in the burgundy leather wing chair opposite Lord Blakestone's. "How can that be right? How can he be married? That's impossible. Wythe's dead."

Hopwood spread his arms…opened his mouth to speak…thought better of it…shook his head in resignation…and walked slowly out of the club.

Every day is

A Mother's Day

in this heartwarming anthology
celebrating motherhood and romance!

Featuring the classic story "Nobody's Child" by Emilie Richards
He had come to a child's rescue, and now Officer Farrell Riley was
suddenly sharing parenthood with beautiful Gemma Hancock.
But would their ready-made family last forever?

Plus two brand-new romances:

"Baby on the Way" by Marie Ferrarella
Single and pregnant, Madeline Reed found the perfect husband in the
handsome cop who helped bring her infant son into the world. But did his
dutiful role in the surprise delivery make J. T. Walker a daddy?

"A Daddy for Her Daughters" by Elizabeth Bevarly
When confronted with spirited Naomi Carmichael and her brood of girls,
bachelor Sloan Sullivan realized he had a lot to learn about women!
Especially if he hoped to win this sexy single mom's heart....

Available this April from Silhouette Books!

Where love comes alive™

COOPER'S  CORNER

In April 2002 you are invited to three wonderful weddings in a very special town...

A Wedding at Cooper's Corner

USA Today **bestselling author**

Kristine Rolofson
Muriel Jensen
Bobby Hutchinson

Ailing Warren Cooper has asked private investigator David Solomon to deliver three precious envelopes to each of his grandchildren. Inside each is something that will bring surprise, betrayal...and unexpected romance!

And look for the exciting launch of *Cooper's Corner*, a NEW 12-book continuity from Harlequin— launching in August 2002.

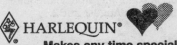

MONTANA
Born

From the bestselling series

MONTANA MAVERICKS

Wed in Whitehorn

Two tales that capture living and loving
beneath the Big Sky.

THE MARRIAGE MAKER by Christie Ridgway

Successful businessman Ethan Redford never proposed a deal he
couldn't close—and that included marriage to Cleo Kincaid Monroe!

AND THE WINNER...WEDS! by Robin Wells

Prim and proper Frannie Hannon yearned for Austin Parker, but
her pearls and sweater sets couldn't catch his boots and jeans—or
could they?

And don't miss

MONTANA
Bred

Featuring

JUST PRETENDING by Myrna Mackenzie

&

STORMING WHITEHORN by Christine Scott

Available in May 2002
Available only from Silhouette at your favorite retail outlet.

Silhouette
Where love comes alive

These New York Times *bestselling authors*
have created stories to capture the hearts and minds
of women everywhere.
Here are three classic tales about the power of love—
and the wonder of discovering the place
where you belong....

FINDING HOME

DUNCAN'S BRIDE
by
LINDA HOWARD

CHAIN LIGHTNING
by
ELIZABETH LOWELL

POPCORN AND KISSES
by
KASEY MICHAELS

Available only from Silhouette
at your favorite retail outlet.

Silhouette®
Where love comes alive™

Silhouette Romance introduces tales of
enchanted love and things beyond explanation
in the new series

Soulmates

Couples destined for each other are brought
together by the powerful magic of love....

A precious gift brings
A HUSBAND IN HER EYES
by Karen Rose Smith (on sale March 2002)

Dreams come true in
CASSIE'S COWBOY
by Diane Pershing (on sale April 2002)

A legacy of love arrives
BECAUSE OF THE RING
by Stella Bagwell (on sale May 2002)

*Available at
your favorite retail outlet.*

Where love comes alive™

Lookin' for some spicy Westerns seasoned
with just the right amount of sizzling
romance and rollicking adventure? Then help
yourselves to these Harlequin Historicals novels

ON SALE MARCH 2002

A MARRIAGE BY CHANCE
by **Carolyn Davidson**
(Wyoming, 1894)

SHADES OF GRAY
by **Wendy Douglas**
(Texas, 1868)

ON SALE APRIL 2002

THE BRIDE FAIR
by **Cheryl Reavis**
(North Carolina, 1868)

THE DRIFTER
by **Lisa Plumley**
(Arizona, 1887)

 Harlequin Historicals®